"For this latest Travelers outing, K[ ] dialogue-driven blast of shifting alliances and action. . . .. With minimal exposition, the author keeps his characters' temperaments and decisions in the forefront of the story. . . .. As always, King leaves his creations in intriguing new positions by the end, ensuring anticipation for the next high-stakes volume. This Travelers tale delivers another exceptional slice of gamesmanship, slippery morals, and emotional fallout."—*Kirkus Reviews*

When the hard men come with their guns. . . and bundle you into the trunk of a car. . . who do you wish had your back?

The Traveling Man and a new partner have their eyes on a safe deposit box full of drug money when the new partner's husband unexpectedly shows up, muddling up the score.

Meanwhile, the Traveling Man's wife, who's busy charming the daughter of her new boyfriend, is spotted by an old mark they previously swindled, a mark who's looking for payback.

The Kidnap Victim is a gritty crime thriller with twist and turns galore. If you like fast-paced action, devious plot twists, and criminal mischief, you'll love the fifth novel in the Travelers series.

THE KIDNAP VICTIM

THE TRAVELERS: BOOK 5

MICHAEL P. KING

BLURRED LINES PRESS

Blurred Lines Press

The Kidnap Victim

Michael P. King

ISBN 978-0-9993648-2-6

Cover design by Paramita Bhattacharjee at creativeparamita.com

The Kidnap Victim is a work of fiction. The names, characters, places, and events are products of the author's imagination or are used fictitiously. Any similarity to real persons or places is entirely coincidental.

For Sarah, my everything

1

ON THEIR OWN

The con man who called himself the Traveling Man, currently going by the name John Ferguson, scooted up the mattress and leaned back against the honey-oak headboard of the bed in his studio apartment in Springville. Light leaked into the room through the gaps in the drapes. It was early on a Saturday afternoon, and he could hear children's voices carrying over from the playground across the parking lot. Once upon a time, this would be the moment to light a cigarette. Instead, he rubbed his gray-streaked beard and glanced down at his new associate, Molly Wright, who smiled up at him before she rolled off the bed and padded across the carpet to the bathroom. She was twenty-five years old, tall and curvy, with long, dark hair that hung down to the middle of her back. She had more confidence than ability, but with his wife, still going by the name Nicole Carter, off playing house with James Denison, he had to make do. If Nicole's relationship with Denison stayed on track, she'd be retiring soon, and he'd need Molly to take her place. He waited for Molly to climb back into bed and arrange the wrinkled sheet around herself before he spoke. "So, did you fuck Robertson or not?"

"I didn't have to."

"You didn't have to? So you teased him, or you promised him, or you led him to believe...What makes you think he's sold?"

"You wanted him thinking with his dick. He's thinking with his dick."

John continued in a casual tone of voice. "No, that's not what I wanted. This is different from the kind of jobs you've pulled before. I want him thinking he's got you. That you're with him. That maybe, even, you might someday love him. In other words, I want him to believe he can trust you. See the difference? You've only been working for him a month. You got to give him a taste. It's a trust thing. It's always about trust. And until you win his trust, he's not going to make you his personal assistant and put you on the safe-deposit-box list. You don't have six months to convince him. You've been flirting him up, haven't you? Giving him the soft sale? Showing him the goods?"

"Yes."

"He put his hands on you."

She nodded.

"In the right places?"

"Yeah."

"And you stopped things how?"

"I did the giggle-shy thing. Told him I couldn't do it in a public place."

"You're very convincing. I'll give you that." John bit his lip. "But can you close the deal?"

She nodded.

"Say it."

"I can do it. No problem."

"Great. The next time you meet, you're going to lock the office door and get the job done. Do you understand?"

"And what are you going to be doing while I'm 'closing the deal'?"

"Everything else. It's never about getting the money; it's always about getting away." He squeezed her hand. "You are coming with me, aren't you?"

"Yes."

"Good." He studied her face carefully. "Now who's that guy I saw you with in the Caffeination Coffee Shop on Thursday? Don't try that clueless look; you can't sell it to me."

She looked him in the eye. "He's an old boyfriend. He's not going to be any trouble. He's only going to be around for a few weeks."

"What's he know?"

"Nothing."

"Really?"

"He just knows I'm working—that he has to stay out of the way."

"Do you believe he can do that, or do I need to talk with him?"

She put her hand on his leg. "Johnny, everything is going to be all right."

"Don't call me Johnny." He moved her hand away. "We're almost there. It's time to get paid. But if Robertson gets spooked, we're all done. We can't have any missteps."

"There won't be any."

"That's all I wanted to hear." He leaned over and kissed her. "Just to be clear. When we leave here, it's just you and me. Your boy is not coming with us. So if he's still in love with you, you need to do whatever you got to do to keep him quiet."

"John—"

"I'm not judging. We've all been there. I'm just saying you've got to take care of it."

MEANWHILE, Nicole was at James Denison's beach house in Cricket Bay, Florida. She and Denison were sitting side by side in matching chaise lounges on the deck of his oval swimming pool, drinking martinis and watching the waves roll up the beach. She was wearing a lime-green bikini and a broad-brimmed hat with a bright, multicolored band. She'd been staying here with Denison for over a month. It had been a little over two months since his wife had died of cancer in Nohamay City, and he'd been caught up in the theft of the Cellini casket. That's where Nicole had met him, first as someone to manipulate, later as an ally. When Denison had asked her to visit, John had told her to go. Now she and Denison were...Was *lovers* too strong a word? Relationships were always so complicated.

"She's not going to like me."

Denison shifted his skinny, sun-browned body toward her. Without the expensive sunglasses on his bearded face and the wedding ring he still wore, he could have passed for a beach bum. "Bell? She's going to love you."

"Jimmy, it's only six weeks since Stacey's funeral. She's going to hate me just as much as she loves her mother."

"That's a little harsh. There's going to be a few bumps until she gets to know you, but trust me, by the time she goes back home, she's going to love you as much as I do."

"Maybe I should leave before she gets here."

"If you want to leave, you can leave, but I want you to stay."

"You've got to think very carefully about how being with me might change your life."

"How's that?"

"You know what I do for a living. You going to tell your kids?"

He sipped from his glass. "Okay. I get it. We've put off talking through the details."

"But now your daughter's on her way, and reality intrudes."

"Can I ask you something personal?"

"Ask away."

"Ron, your business partner..."

"He goes by John, now."

"Okay, John. How close is your relationship?"

"What do you mean?"

"Do you sleep with him?"

She laughed. "You really do want to get personal. I always have. Why? Does that bother you?"

"I don't know. How does he feel about you being here?"

"He told me I should come."

"So he doesn't care that you're sleeping with me?"

She shook her head.

"Do you love him?"

"We have a long history together. I know I can count on him no matter what. This may sound kind of weird, but he makes me stronger. Not like I'm depending on him, but..."

"I know exactly what you mean. Stacey made me stronger. And better." Denison's voice cracked. A broken smile crept across his face. "So if he's your center, why are you here with me?"

Nicole set her glass on the deck. "Are you having a good time? I'm having a good time. I checked my cares and worries at your front door, and I hope I'm helping you to do the same." She rolled off her chaise lounge and onto Denison. His martini sloshed out of his glass. She kissed him hard. "Am I driving you crazy in a good way? 'Cause that's my nefarious plan."

"I just want—"

"Shush." She put her finger on his lips. "No more talking. I care about you, James. I want to be with you. That's why I'm here. But tomorrow your daughter comes, and I move to the guest bedroom. So let's make the best of today."

BACK IN SPRINGVILLE, Molly stood at the tan Formica countertop that separated the kitchen from the living room in her one-bedroom apartment, a half lime on the cutting board in front of her and a vodka tonic in her hand. Her husband, Chad, sat in the living room on the gray rent-to-own sofa, drinking a beer from the bottle.

"I'm not going to tell you about that," she said.

"Why not?" Chad stood up. He was over six feet, with a crooked nose and muddy-brown hair cropped short around the sides. He was dressed in khaki pants, moccasins, and a red golf shirt. He looked like a happy-go-lucky fraternity brother.

"We've been over this."

"Because John will find out? How's that going to happen?"

"You'll start nosing around, and he'll see you."

"Please."

"He saw us together at the Caffeination."

"What did you tell him?"

"Old boyfriend who was just in town for a few weeks."

"Good. That gives me a little room to work."

"You're not working."

"Whatever you got going must have something to do with that lawyer you work for. We could squeeze him tomorrow and be on our way."

"That's a no-money play compared to what John and I have been building. We've never seen a score this big."

"But there's no guarantee that it's going to happen."

"Be patient and stay out of the way. John knows what he's doing."

"We don't have that much time."

"I'm not the one who got those detectives after us. I've been here working for almost a month, okay? Stay out of sight and give me a few more days."

Chad walked over to the countertop. "You seem a little confused about your loyalties. It's me and you against the world."

"I know."

"You think John won't try to cheat you out of your end when the time is right? I'm the guy who's watching your back."

She grasped his free hand and leaned over the counter to bring her face close to his. "Chad, I'm your girl. I'm leaving here with you. Just give me a little more time to finish this up."

"Okay, then."

"Okay." She closed her eyes and kissed him. "Lighten up. You've got nothing to worry about."

THE NEXT DAY Nicole stood on the deck of the swimming pool behind Denison's beach house. She was wearing a translucent, hip-length beach cover-up over her bikini. The sun was hot. From where she stood, she had an excellent view of the surf rolling up the beach. She heard the car door slam. James was back from the airport with his daughter, Bell, a thirty-year-old art history professor. Nicole took a deep breath. She had to play this just right. She'd chosen this particular bikini because it cut across her hips in a way that made her flesh sag ever so slightly, and even though she usually passed for late thirties, she'd applied her makeup to make herself look closer to her actual age of forty-five. There was even a touch of gray in her shoulder-length, auburn hair. James wouldn't notice, of course, but Bell would focus on every detail. She was expecting a young beauty with her claws into her vulnerable, infatuated old dad. What Nicole wanted her to begin to see was a middle-aged woman who could be good company for him. From her very first words, she needed to capture just the right level of intimacy: the friend of the father, but not the replacement mother; the familiar guest, not the mistress of the house.

Bell and James came through the swimming pool gate together. He'd put on a blue blazer over his golf clothes for the trip to the airport. Bell was a tall woman of about five ten, with long, wavy, red hair. She wore a white linen pantsuit with a floral-pattern shirt. Nicole thought she looked much like her mother—pretty in a practical way. Bell smiled a plastic smile and stuck out her hand. "So you're Nicki?"

"Nicole." They exchanged a job interview handshake. "How was your flight?"

"Uneventful." She glanced at the drinks tray sitting on the circular white table in the shade of the red-striped umbrella. She turned to her father. "Dad, are we sitting out here by the pool?"

"I thought we might."

"I'd rather stay out of the sun. Is that okay with you, Nicole?"

"Sure."

"How about in the den by the windows?"

Denison nodded. Bell slipped her arm through his and steered him toward the patio door. "I'd forgotten how much I missed this place, Dad."

"It's great to have you here, honey."

"Next time maybe Bobby will be able to come."

"It's a shame he couldn't get away."

Nicole watched them enter the house and then picked up the

drinks tray and followed them. Bell hadn't wasted any time elbowing out her place in the pecking order. So far, so good.

The den was situated at the end of the house, its east wall filled by a row of large, double-hung windows. Bell sat down next to her father on the sofa facing the windows. Nicole set the drinks tray on the glass-topped coffee table and sat in a chair diagonal to them, so they shared the same view of the ocean. She sat back in the chair, her arms beside her, as if she were the clueless guest waiting for someone else to take charge, not the woman who had been running the house for the last month.

Denison scooted forward. "I'm so glad you two are getting the chance to meet. Would you like a drink, Bell?"

"Day drinking, Dad? Are you okay?"

Denison smiled awkwardly and glanced toward Nicole, but she didn't say a word. "Just celebrating your arrival, honey."

"Well, if it's a celebration, let's have champagne."

Denison stood up. "That's a great idea. I think there's a bottle in the fridge. Nicole, could you help me with the glasses?"

"Where are they?"

He pointed to a built-in cabinet on the wall to their right. "I think they're somewhere in there." He turned to Bell. "Do you remember where?"

Bell shrugged.

Nicole made a show of searching through the cabinet while Denison retrieved the bottle. "Did you find them?" he asked.

"Finally," she said. She brought three champagne flutes back to the coffee table.

Denison worked the cork out of the bottle with a satisfying pop, poured, and passed around the glasses. "What shall we toast?"

Bell held her glass up. "To Mom. May she always be in our hearts."

Nicole politely raised her glass. She had to admire Bell's strategy. She couldn't compete with the dead wife and mother. This was going to be a tough couple of weeks.

Denison paused for a moment, then raised his glass. "To

your mom."

LATER THAT AFTERNOON, the tide receding down the shore and the sun far to the west, Denison and Bell were walking barefoot along the beach in the damp zone between the rushing waves and the dry sand. Bell had changed into a long, loose sundress, and Denison wore a T-shirt and old cargo shorts. "Dad, I know you're lonely, that you miss Mom, that Nicole and her partner—whatever that means—helped you out at Nohamay City. I still don't really understand what happened there."

"Long story short, you remember how your mother loved Cellini's work? I was trying to buy a jewelry casket for her. Beautiful little box. Turned out it was stolen. Nicole and John kept me from getting into trouble."

"John? That's her partner?"

Denison nodded.

"What's he like?"

"He's one of those hard-nosed business types. Easy to get along with if you're on the same side. But not the kind of guy you'd want to cross."

"And what's their business?"

"Nicole would have to explain that to you."

Bell looked at him over the top of her sunglasses. "Why? Why can't you just tell me?"

"Because you have to ask her."

"This is exactly the kind of thing that has me and Skip worried, Dad. You've only known her a few months, and you're thick as thieves. Don't you think it's too soon to get involved in a serious relationship?"

Denison picked up a flat stone and sailed it into the surf. "It's not serious."

"Not serious? You emailed me and Skip that she was moving in."

Denison smiled and shook his head. "I know you and your brother are just concerned that it's only been a couple of months since your mom passed, and that's why I'm not mad. Reread the email. I said she was visiting."

"She's been living here for a month."

"I asked her to come out; she doesn't have anywhere to stay; of course she's going to stay at the house. She has her own room."

"Since I got here."

He shrugged. "Fair enough. But I'm still your dad. I don't have to explain myself to you. You're just going to have to trust me. I'm going slow. I haven't given her anything and she hasn't asked for anything, if that's what you're worried about. It's just that right now I just need someone who's only for me."

"Only for you? There's nobody like that, Dad."

"Give her a chance. A real chance. I think you'll like her."

"Dad, what do you really know about her? I mean real, verifiable fact. What do you know?"

THAT EVENING, Nicole, Denison, and Bell sat at a candlelit table in Jerry's Surf House, a seafood restaurant located in the old village by the docks. It was decorated in a pirate motif. Fishing nets, fake swords, treasure maps, and black skull and crossbones flags hung from the walls. The restaurant was Sunday-evening empty, the vacationing families having come and gone earlier, and the weekend visitors already on the road headed for home. Nicole, Denison, and Bell were lingering after their meal, sipping coffee and enjoying the quiet.

"I told you this was still the best restaurant in town," Denison said.

"And still the kitschiest," Bell replied. "Remember when they had the skeleton hanging up between the doors to the restrooms?"

Denison chuckled. "Your brother wouldn't go to the bathroom by himself."

"How long have you been coming here?" Nicole asked.

Bell shrugged. "We've always come here."

"We bought the beach house back before all the development," Denison said. "The businesses on the highway, the access road, the chain restaurants—all that came later. This was a sleepy village. And this restaurant was one of its best-kept secrets. The kids grew up coming here—what? Two or three times a year?"

Bell nodded. "Mom loved this place. She liked the beach here better than the beach in California."

He nodded. "Of course, Bell and Skip come out here whenever they want now."

"Really?" Nicole said. "That must be nice."

"I hardly have the time," Bell said. "And then when I do go on vacation, I want to try something new. I haven't been here in two years."

"Well, at least you got a chance to come down before school starts," Denison said. "The season will be over in a few more weeks and things will quiet down around here."

"What are you teaching this fall?" Nicole asked.

"Three classes," Bell replied. "Two I taught last fall, but I'm having to revamp my Intro to Western European, so it's going to be a lot of work getting all the new images prepared." She turned to her father. "So how much longer are you planning to stay out here, Dad?"

Denison looked down at his coffee cup. "Honestly, I don't know. I've been avoiding the Palo Alto house. Not sure if I'm ready for all the memories of your mom. But Jody called from the Institute. I should be there making sure the fall kickoff starts strong."

"The homeless women's program?" Nicole asked.

"Yeah," Denison said. "A lot of the women are moms, so we have a big fund-raiser that coincides with the start of school."

"It will do you good to do some work," Bell said.

"You're probably right."

"And Angela can help you with Mom's stuff, unless you want to wait for Thanksgiving break."

"Angela shouldn't have to do it."

"Then I'll fly out in November."

"Maybe I should just sell the Palo Alto place, move into San Francisco for a change."

"You don't have to decide now. You could rent something in town.

Then you'd be able to start on the fund-raiser without thinking about the house, and you could make up your mind later."

"True enough."

Bell turned to Nicole. "And how about you? Have you got any plans for the fall?"

Nicole shook her head. "Not yet. I haven't heard anything from my partner, and as long as he doesn't need me..."

"And what is it you do for work?"

"It's difficult to explain."

"Try me."

"We rob criminals."

"You're joking." She turned to her father. "That's what she told you?"

He nodded.

Nicole continued. "That's what he's seen us do. We crossed paths in the process of recovering a stolen object. The Cellini casket. Maybe you heard the news report about its return. James fell into the middle of it. We helped him out."

"How?"

"Proved to him it was stolen. Helped him avoid a charge of receiving stolen property."

Denison squeezed Nicole's hand. "If you're not busy, you should just come out to California with me. There's plenty for us to do."

"Dad," Bell said, "she can't put her life on hold forever to keep you company."

Nicole smiled. "It's sweet of you to be concerned about me, but there's nothing I'd rather do than be with your father."

Bell let out an exasperated sigh, and then caught herself. "Sorry. I just..."

"Let's change the subject and get the check," Denison said.

OUTSIDE, a warm salt wind was blowing off the ocean, and a few clouds skittered across the night sky. Nicole was walking across the well-lit parking lot in front of Jerry's Surf House with Denison and

Bell. They were halfway to their Ford Explorer when a voice called out.

"Sally. Sally Jones. That's you, isn't it?"

Nicole turned. A fat man with a thin comb-over and jug-handle ears was gaining on them. It was Fred Stein. How long ago had it been? He'd put on weight.

"Don't deny it," he said. "You're Sally Jones. Are these your partners—the ones I never met—or are you running a con on them?"

"You're talking crazy, mister." She stepped back. Denison moved up beside her. "Don't come any closer or I'm calling the police," she said.

Bell backed up against a parked Nissan Sentra. "What makes you think she's this person you know?"

Stein looked Nicole over. "The hair is different. The clothes are different. Even your manner is different. But you're definitely Sally. You cheated me out of sixty thousand dollars."

"I don't know you," Nicole said.

"How long ago was this?" Bell asked.

"Five years." He turned to Nicole. "Knock it off, Sally. You know who I am."

"Five years ago," Nicole said. "I had different hair, different clothes. I acted differently. That sounds like I was a different person. Why do you think I'm her?" She didn't wait for him to answer. "I'm calling the police."

Stein stared hard at her face. "You're calling the police?"

"Right now." She started tapping the screen on her phone.

Stein muttered something and sighed. "I guess I must be wrong. My mistake. Sorry." He turned away.

They continued across the lot to the Explorer. "Sorry about that," Nicole said. "Occupational hazard."

"You did know him?" Bell asked.

"He went to jail for stealing credit card information, which is why he didn't want the police involved."

"That guy was a crook?"

"Yeah, I know. Hard to believe, isn't it?"

"So you've worked here before, scamming criminals?" Bell asked.

"Never. I've never been here before. This is the kind of place we go to in between jobs. Never work and play in the same place."

Denison unlocked the SUV with the key fob. "That sounds like one of John's rules."

Nicole nodded. "One of a long list."

FRED STEIN WATCHED the three as they continued across the parking lot. He looked directly at the brunette, studying her, watching the way she blinked, turned her head, smiled. How could he have been wrong? She was the spitting image of Sally Jones, the swindler who'd cheated him out of $60,000 and put the police on him. He'd never been arrested before, but he got two years in prison for stealing those credit card numbers. He hadn't been able to get an IT job anywhere since he got out. He'd slept with Sally for three weeks, and he'd never suspected a thing. The brunette shrugged her shoulders and swiveled her hips as she reached for the Ford Explorer's door handle. An image of Sally Jones opening a car door the last time he saw her flashed through his mind. It was her. There was no doubt about it. God, she was convincing.

He jogged over to his Toyota Corolla and backed out of his parking space just in time to follow them out of the lot. They took a right onto Campbell Street and then another right onto Lighthouse Boulevard. Traffic was sparse, and the full moon lit up the road, so he dropped back about a city block, watching their taillights. When they turned left into Sandy Run Estates, he followed. They were in one of the old, upscale neighborhoods now, palm trees and iron gates. What were they doing? Casing a house for a robbery? He watched them pull into a driveway and park in the garage. He pulled over on the opposite side of the street and wrote down the address before he made a wide circle and drove away.

His cell phone rang. It was his wife.

"Carrie, I was just about to call you."

"How was your day?"

"Long. How was yours?"

"I caught a double. Just got home. Timmy and Lori stayed at my mom's."

"You must be dead."

"My feet are killing me. But I made enough in tips to pay the school supply fees. How did your interview go?"

"I think it went pretty well," he lied. "I'm supposed to hear back in two days."

"I've got my fingers crossed."

"Me too."

"You coming home tomorrow?"

"I've got another lead, so it may be a few more days."

"That's great. What is it?"

"Another office equipment maintenance job. I've got to hustle if I hope to get an interview."

"You'll get one."

"I hope so."

"Well, I've got the breakfast shift tomorrow, so I need to go to bed. Just wanted to hear your voice."

"Kiss the kids for me."

"I will. I love you."

"I love you too."

Stein pulled into the parking lot of the Ocean Surf Inn. He had to find a job, and he couldn't lie about his prison record. When they'd found out about it on his last job, they'd fired him on the spot. Not even an "I'm sorry" or a "We know you were a good worker." Jesus. One mistake. Carrie waiting tables. No health insurance. And the mortgage falling further and further behind. Pretty soon they'd be getting an eviction notice. He watched a family get out of their car and walk into the motel. Mom and dad holding hands. The two middle schoolers laughing and running ahead. Vacationers. Making carefree memories together. What was that like? He deserved that. His family deserved that.

He got out of his car. Sally Jones. How strange was it running into her? He took out his phone. He needed to talk to someone who knew the whole story. He found Rudy Grissom's number in his contacts list. "Rudy? It's Fred. You'll never guess who I ran into."

Grissom sighed. "Okay, I'll humor you. Who did you run into?"

"Sally Jones."

"The bitch who conned you? Come on, Fred, that was, what? Five years easy. How can you be sure?"

"It was her all right. I confronted her."

"What did she say?"

"She denied it. But I'm telling you, it's her. I followed her back to the house she's staying at."

"Why did you do that?"

"To see if she's up to something."

"Why?"

"Maybe I can get her into trouble."

"Fred, how can you be sure it's really her?"

"She was my girlfriend, remember?"

"Don't start something you can't control, that's all I'm saying. How did the job interview go?"

"As soon as they found out about my conviction, it was over."

"Tough break, man. If you need the money, I can put you on here at the club until you find something else."

"Doorman at a gentlemen's club? I appreciate the offer, but really, Rudy, I'd just look silly."

"Suit yourself."

"Catch you later."

"Keep your head down."

Stein headed into the motel. Sally Jones living in an upscale neighborhood. It didn't make sense. As soon as he got up to his room, he was going to do an Internet search and find out who owned that house.

NICOLE, Denison, and Bell got out of the SUV in the garage and entered the house through the mudroom, turning on lights as they went. "It's so hard to believe," Bell said.

"There's a lot of people in this world who believe they deserve to get something for nothing," Nicole replied.

"Don't you think that's kind of cynical?" Bell asked.

"Just my experience." Nicole walked into the kitchen. "White wine?"

"Nothing for me," Denison said.

Nicole took the bottle from the refrigerator and waved it around. Bell held up her thumb and index finger to indicate a small amount. Nicole poured wine for both of them and handed a glass to Bell.

"So how do you find out about these people?" Bell asked.

"Sometimes they find us."

"And you make friends with them."

"You can call it that."

"Then you steal what they've stolen and put them in jail."

"Sometimes."

"But the people who were robbed to begin with..."

"Not my problem. They're usually culpable anyway." Nicole leaned back against the counter and sipped her wine.

"How's that?"

"In the case of the guy we just saw, he was stealing credit-card info from a grocery store chain. How is that possible? The grocery store chain didn't want to pay for the protection they needed, so they put their customers at risk. If they had done the right thing to begin with, their customers, and their customers' banks, would have been safe. As it was, we exposed the problem, which was then fixed. Crazy, huh?"

"But you kept the money?"

"Yeah. That's how we make a living."

"It's still hard to believe."

Denison nodded. "I'd have a hard time believing it too, if I hadn't been pulled into that scam in Nohamay City. I was so preoccupied with your mom that I thought I was dealing with a legitimate seller. If Nicole and John hadn't realized I'd been duped, I could have been on the evening news."

Bell put her glass on the counter by the sink. "I'm going to turn in." She hugged her father. "Good to see you, Dad."

"I'm glad you're here," he said.

Denison waited for Bell to leave the room before he spoke to Nicole. "See, I told you she'd warm up after she got to know you."

"Maybe," Nicole replied.

"Do we need to be worried about that guy?"

"Fred Stein? I don't think so. He seemed more pitiful than dangerous."

Denison reached for her hand. "You coming to bed?"

She smiled. "Don't we have to keep up appearances for Bell's sake?"

"She's a heavy sleeper."

"Let's let her settle in a bit first."

BELL, her red hair tied back in a loose ponytail, stood naked in her bathroom, rubbing lotion on her arms and legs. Nothing was as she'd expected it to be. She'd been imagining a younger woman, a casino divorcee in flashy clothes who'd cast a spell over her father that she'd be able to see right through. Instead, Nicole seemed genuine, authentic, as if she really did care about Dad. And Dad was obviously in love with her. It hurt so much. And was she really telling the truth about her work? Who would claim to be a thief if they weren't? The situation was much more complicated than what she and Skip had talked about. What time was it? She wondered what Bobby was doing. She pulled her nightgown on over her head and picked up her phone from the counter on her way into the bedroom. She climbed into bed in the dark with her phone in her hand and called home. The phone rang again and again. She was ready to leave a message when Bobby finally picked up. "Hello?"

"It's me, honey. It's not too late, is it? I didn't wake you?"

"It's okay," he said. "I was just dreaming about my other girlfriend."

"I bet. How was your day?"

"Pretty standard. Finished writing the final exam for my class.

Spent the rest of the afternoon working on that paper I've got to give next month. Ate the leftover lasagna for supper. How's your trip going so far?"

"Well, I met Nicole..."

He chuckled. "Tell all. What is she—twenty-three, twenty-four?"

"Actually, she doesn't look that much younger than Mom."

"Really? So what's she like?"

"Hard to tell. She's nice and all. Really pretty. She's got Dad wrapped around her finger, but she doesn't act like it. The crazy thing is that she and her partner, some guy named John, are scammers who go after criminals."

"What?"

"While we were at dinner, a stranger accused her of having robbed him five years ago. He backed down after she threatened to call the police."

"You've got to be kidding."

"No. And that's not even the crazy part. She had robbed the guy. The guy was stealing credit card information. They stole his money and got him arrested."

"So your dad is having an affair with a beautiful, middle-aged career criminal. What are you going to do?"

"I don't know. Skip thinks I can just wave my magic wand, and Dad will dump her." She shifted onto her side. "I wish you were here with me."

"I wish you were here in bed with me, and I'm glad I'm not there. If your brother has a problem with what your dad is doing, he should talk to your dad himself instead of dumping the problem on you."

"You just don't get it. Dad really loved Mom. He was a wreck. He wouldn't give up on her even when it was hopeless. You saw him. There's just no way he's in a place where he's making good decisions."

"Don't get angry with me. That's why I'm glad I'm not there. It's your family. You guys have to work it out."

"I don't mean to snap at you. It's just so frustrating."

"You've got over two weeks to figure things out. Take your time. I'm sure you'll have a better sense of things in a few days."

2

CLOSING THE DEAL

On Monday, Molly was back at work at the offices of Neil Robertson, Attorney at Law. She'd spent the morning in the workroom, running copies and assembling packets for a complicated divorce case and keeping an eye on the door to Robertson's private office. She'd expected him to slip into the workroom to chat her up and paw her, but he hadn't appeared. Betty, the receptionist, a motherly middle-aged blonde who kept a jar of candy on her desk, poked her head in. "How's it going?"

"Almost done."

"I'm going to lunch."

Molly placed the last documents into the packets. It was time for her to make her move. She was wearing a lacey pink bra and thong set under a tailored gray skirt and a cream-colored blouse that was tight across the bust. This was the first time she'd ever set up a mark when she was sober, but she couldn't risk booze on her breath when she moved in close to him. She was just going to have to rely on her instinct. How hard could it be? Guys like Robertson were grabby even when they didn't think they were. She unbuttoned the top button of her blouse, picked up a document that needed his signature, and strolled into his office. Robertson looked up from his laptop, a quizzical expression on his face. He was a thin man with a shaved head and a round potbelly that stretched the front of his blue shirt. She didn't say a word; she just came around his oak desk, leaned down beside him, and set the document in front of him. "This needs your signature."

When Robertson turned to look up at her, he was looking straight into her cleavage. He leered up at her through his Van Dyke beard. "Betty gone to lunch?"

Molly tried to look coy. "She just left."

He stood up and pushed her back onto the corner of his desk. Her hands were on the desk behind her. He leaned into her and kissed her. "You're not teasing me anymore." He started unbuttoning her blouse.

Molly glanced over her shoulder. "The door." She slipped out of his grasp, sauntered to the door and locked it. "That's better."

She porn-star walked back to him, put her arms around his neck and kissed him slowly. He motioned toward the black leather sofa under the built-in bookshelves.

After he finished, he climbed off her, pulled up his boxer shorts and pants all together, and began buttoning his shirt. She sat up on the sofa and straightened her thong. That had been easier than she thought. She stood up and turned her back to him while she hooked her bra and tucked in her blouse. She was fumbling in her mind for something to say.

"That was fun," Robertson said.

She looked over her shoulder and smiled. She'd never been with a man who finished so fast.

He grinned. "I hope this is the start of something good for both of us."

"Me too."

He sat back down behind his desk. "You need to go to lunch before Betty gets back and finds out you never left. She's known my wife for years. We can't have any gossip in the office."

"Sure thing." Molly unlocked the door and left if slightly ajar. She smiled to herself. There she was. One step closer to the safe-deposit box.

ROBERTSON WATCHED her ass wiggle as she walked out of the room. She was a tasty bit, soft and round in all the right places. How had it taken him a whole month to get her onto his sofa? Girls didn't come any simpler than her. Thought she was seducing him. Now he'd be able to get more work out of her on the promise of advancing her career. Like that could ever happen. But at least he could have fun screwing her until she figured things out. And he'd be able to send her on little errands that he needed to keep on the down low. That fawning look in her eye told him everything he needed to know.

He picked up his desk phone and called home. "Honey? How's your day? I'm going to be a little late for supper."

MOLLY SAT in a booth at the Chicos Verde Mexican restaurant across the street from Roberson's offices, a half-eaten burrito in front of her, talking on the phone with John. The dining room was plastered to look like yellow adobe. A row of giant sombreros ran around the top of the walls and a red-and-green stripe accented the yellow paint. The dining room was full. The Mexican music, the clatter of dishes, and the cacophony of voices provided the perfect background for a discreet conversation.

"Did you get it done?" John asked.

"Yes."

"Walk me through the details."

She described what happened.

"Excellent. I knew you had it in you."

"He's just wham, bam, thank you, ma'am."

"Less work for you."

"Can I ask you something?"

"Sure."

"How do you know that screwing him is the right play? Why won't he just see right through it?"

"It doesn't always work. The mark has to believe that he has the power, and that he deserves the sex. If he does, he's less likely to be suspicious. Then most guys tend to feel closer to a woman they're sleeping with—or at least think they have more control over her. *Voila*. Increased likelihood of intimacy, which in the workplace leads to trust."

"So even though he's cheating on his wife—"

"Emotionally he's a clueless bastard, which is why this con works. Coming at him with a deal would get his mind working, which, in his case, would make the chance of success much lower."

"He hasn't put me on the safe-deposit-box list yet."

"He will. We just have to wait him out. He'll need to put something in the box, he won't want to go, and he'll send you. Anything else?"

"No."

"Great job."

She put away her phone. She felt like celebrating, bragging a little, but she couldn't tell Chad. He'd be jealous, maybe angry. She still had thirty minutes before she had to be back at the office. One drink wouldn't hurt. She signaled to her server, a young Latino in a white shirt and new jeans. "A margarita, please."

NICOLE LAY in her bikini on a chaise lounge on the deck by the pool, sunning herself and reading the current issue of *The Atlantic* magazine. Bell came out through the patio door in a sleeveless sundress. She looked off in the distance for a moment, and then down at Nicole as if she hadn't noticed her before. "Have you seen my dad?"

Nicole lowered her magazine. "He's at the golf course. There's three guys in the neighborhood he plays with twice a week. They usually play first thing in the morning, but somebody had a conflict." She looked at the clock on the face of her smart phone. "He should be back in about an hour."

Bell dragged over a chair from the umbrella table and sat down. "Good. This gives us a chance to talk privately."

Nicole adjusted her chaise lounge to a more upright position. "What's on your mind?"

Bell rolled her eyes. "I can't believe I'm doing this, but here goes. I don't know you. It looks like you make my dad happy, but I'm telling you that I'm watching you. Dad's in a fragile place right now. He had a hard time dealing with my mom's cancer, and my brother and I want to make sure he isn't hurt or taken advantage of."

"I understand. Your father's relationship with me must seem awfully sudden to you."

"Sudden? That doesn't begin to cover it."

"Have I done anything that makes you uneasy?"

"That man last night, your explanation of your work—quite frankly, it scares the hell out of me."

"Fair enough. But is there anything I've done so far concerning your father?"

"I wish there was. It would make everything easier."

Nicole smiled. "Because absence of evidence isn't evidence of absence." She set her feet on the deck and leaned toward Bell. "Let me put my cards on the table, since that's what we seem to be doing. Your dad is a great guy. I've never met anyone quite like him. Our time together is very special to me. I would never do anything to hurt him. And I hope you and your brother will eventually see that."

"How much longer are you planning on staying?"

"Just like I said last night, I don't know. I hadn't really thought about it. As long as John doesn't need me, and James wants me around, I don't have any plans. But I'm going to be honest with you. That man turning up last night could be a hiccup. If he shows up again, I may have to leave for a bit."

"Because?"

"Because I don't want anyone bothering your dad."

AT THE GOLDMINER'S CLUB, Fred Stein's friend Rudy Grissom, a blocky, gray-haired man with an acne-scarred face and a confident smile, sat at a small table with two of the bouncers he supervised. Kevin Johnson was a large black man with a one-inch Afro and pirate earrings, and Chris Billings was an amateur boxer with spiky blond hair and a permanent scowl. The club wasn't open yet. The lights were up and a dark-haired dancer in red lingerie and an open turquoise robe was vacuuming in the back of the room. "You guys remember Fred?"

"Clueless white guy you know from prison?" Johnson asked.

"The very one. I think maybe he's found us a score. He just doesn't know it yet."

"Thought he was going straight."

"Yeah, so did he. But he's broke. Can't find a job."

"What's the score?" Billings asked.

"Not sure about the details yet. Might be ripping off a scam."

"Really?"

"He wants to get back at the woman who sent him to jail."

"How would that work?" Billings asked.

"She's a player," Grissom said. "She can't go to the police. He thinks she's on a job."

"Cool," Johnson said. "When will you know if there's something in it for us?"

"Just have to wait and see. If this score comes together, I want him to think it's his idea and I'm just his wingman."

"So what's the real plan?"

"If it pans out, we'll stiff Fred and take all the money."

"Count me in," Billings said.

Johnson chuckled. "You're a real bastard, Rudy."

Grissom shrugged. "Some guys are just meant to get screwed, and Fred is one of them."

CHAD WRIGHT PULLED into the parking lot of the Budget Host Inn. He was driving his truck with his right hand, listening to a country station on the radio, and working a toothpick between his teeth with his left. As he drove by the office door, he thought he saw a car that looked familiar—a black Impala with a Georgia license plate. He craned his head for a second, but he didn't stop. He drove down to the parking space in front of room 124 and pulled in. The *Do Not Disturb* sign was still on his door. The toothpick he'd slipped between the door and jamb below the lock was still in place. He glanced up and down the sidewalk nonchalantly; then he walked down to the office until he could see through the window. A heavy-set man in a tan suit and a white cowboy hat was standing at the counter. *Damn.*

Chad hurried back down to his room and grabbed the packed suitcase that he'd left on the bed. The Impala was still in front of the offices when he got back into his truck. He drove to the end of the lot, turned right into the alley behind the hotel, and then turned left into the Perkins Restaurant parking lot. The traffic light at the intersection was turning green as he bounced over the curb and onto the street. A block later, he turned into a residential neighborhood. No one was following him, but he randomly circled a few blocks, just in case, before he drove toward the beltway ramp. He got out his phone. "Molly? A detective tracked me to the motel."

"Are you sure?"

"Yeah. It was one of the guys that found me last time."

"Where are you now?"

"I'm on the interstate. They must be tracking this truck."

"You need to trade it in."

"We need to get out of here."

"I can't leave. The last piece of the puzzle fell into place today. Any day now, this deal is going to pop. Then we'll leave here with more money than we've ever seen at one time. Those detectives will never be able to find us. Get rid of the truck, find another motel, and stay out of sight."

"Why can't I just stay at your place?"

"Because John will find out."

"How? I'll stay inside. Even your neighbors won't know I'm there."

"Trust me. He'll know. The closer we get to the money, the more careful he's become. God knows what he would do if he thought I fucked up the plan."

"Who cares? He's an old guy. I can take him."

"Just get rid of the truck and find a new motel."

MOLLY HUNG UP HER PHONE. She looked out the door of her office into the reception area. Betty wasn't at her desk. Goddamn Randy Mitchell. She wished she'd never met him in that hotel bar and gone up to his room. He seemed like easy money. They'd taken his rings and watch and the cash from his wallet. There was no reason for Chad to beat him down. The guy hadn't hurt her. She'd been drunk, of course. The scene was blurry in her mind. Chad crashed into the room just as she'd fallen down. Randy was standing over her, reaching down to help her up. She could never figure out if Chad had lost his temper or just made a mistake. The result was the same. Private detectives hunting them.

Up until that incident, she'd never questioned her relationship with Chad. Even if he was impulsive and could be overconfident, they'd always been good together. But after working with John, she saw her possibilities differently. He'd shown her how easy it was to fool a mark if your research was good. What more could she learn if she stuck with him? But leaving Chad was a big step. He definitely had her back. He'd proven it over and over again, even when there was no money on the table. John? She was his new girl. She felt sure that he would be there for her if there was still a chance to score the cash, but there was no history between them for him to step up if the money was gone. Fucking him wasn't going to make him sentimental. At least not in the beginning.

Molly watched Betty sit down at her desk and turn on her computer. She turned to her own computer screen. Should she play it safe or take a chance on something new? Would Chad come after her if she left with John? Probably. How would John react if that happened? Would he shoot first or turn on the charm? She'd feel bad if Chad got hurt, but how bad and for how long? As soon as she and

John had the safe-deposit-box key, she was going to have to decide who she was going to leave with.

LATER THAT EVENING Stein was sitting in his car in the half-empty parking lot of the Cup-N-Sup restaurant. Carrie hadn't sounded too disappointed when he told her he got the form rejection email instead of the second interview, but that was because she thought he had another job lead. Why had he lied to her? He had to find a job with health insurance and retirement benefits. He had to make enough money to catch up the mortgage. But how could he make that happen? No one was hiring ex-cons to work around computers, and that was all he knew how to do. He watched an elderly couple totter out of the restaurant. It was all her fault. Fucking Sally Jones. He'd checked the property records. The house in Sandy Run Estates belonged to James Denison. He'd seen a picture of him on the Internet. He was definitely the guy with Sally in the parking lot. And he was rich. Didn't even have a job. She had to be conning him. How much money was she taking him for? Stein watched the elderly couple get into an old Buick. Why shouldn't Sally have to pay him back? His phone rang. It was Rudy Grissom. "What's up?"

"You still down there in Cricket Bay?"

"Yeah."

"What did you find out about Sally?"

"It turns out that house she was going in belongs to the guy she was with."

"So maybe she isn't Sally Jones."

"It was her. I'm just not sure what her game is, but I know she's up to something. I'm going to figure out what it is."

"Why? That just sounds like a plan for driving yourself crazy."

"Maybe I could get my money back."

"Get your money back? Are you serious?"

"I need time to find a decent job. That money could buy me the time."

"But how do you know she's going to have the money?"

"She's conning somebody. She's going to get paid."

"Fred, listen to yourself. Do you really want to do this?"

"My family's counting on me. She put me in this hole. She deserves to pay."

"You're taking a big risk."

"It's no risk. She's a grifter. She can't tell anyone."

"We're just talking about the money, not some bullshit revenge?"

"Just the money."

The line was quiet for a moment. "You sure?"

"I'm sure."

"Okay, maybe I can help you out."

"Really? You'd do that for me?"

"We're talking about the money. Nothing else."

"Just the money."

"How're you going to do it?"

"I'll follow her around until I find out what she's up to. Then I'll call you to come help. As soon as she gets paid, we'll rob her."

"We'll need more guys than just us."

"Are you sure? We've got to keep this quiet."

"And we will. But if you want to take her score, we need at least two more guys."

"What's that going to cost? I want my sixty thousand back."

"Okay. You want your sixty. I got no problem with that. I need thirty for helping you."

"Thirty thousand? That much?"

"Hey, organizing the people and buying the guns is a lot of work. If it blows up, I'll be the one facing the ATF charges."

"We've got to have guns?"

"You want to be sure? We don't want to be the only people there without any guns."

"So it's ninety thousand."

"And I ought to be able to get two guys to help at five grand apiece. So that's a total of one hundred grand."

"Christ, Rudy, forty grand to do the job. That's a lot of money."

"You want the job done right?"

"I just want to get my money back."

"This is how it happens."

"You sure you can get two guys at five grand apiece?"

"You sure we can get one hundred thousand?"

"That's pencil dust to Denison. Sally's got to be conning him for a lot more than that."

"Okay, then. Let me get to work on the guys and the guns."

"I'll let you know as soon as I find out anything. And Rudy, thanks for helping me out. It means a lot."

"No problem, bro."

Stein started his car. A few minutes ago getting his money back had just been wishful thinking. Now a plan was falling into place. How had that happened? He pulled out of the Cup-N-Sup parking lot. It was the right thing to do. As long as the plan was just about ripping off Sally, and no one else was involved, no one would know. He'd get away clean, he'd find a job, the mortgage would be caught up, and Carrie could quit work. They'd be a happy family again, just like he'd never gone to prison. He'd stay on the straight and narrow. Ten years from now, his conviction would just be a blip in the road. It was a good thing that he'd kept up with Rudy. He was a real pal.

NICOLE AND DENISON lay naked in the dark on the silk sheets of his king-size bed. The window curtains were open. They could see the stars twinkling in the night sky, and even though the windows were closed, they could hear the surf crashing against the shore. Nicole shifted onto her side and lay her head on his chest. He stroked her hair.

"I'm so glad that Bell's bedroom is at the other end of the hall," she whispered.

He nodded. "It's just too soon to try to explain."

"I understand."

"They weren't there in Nohamay City. If they were, they'd know."

"When you're locked in a crucible with a person, you either come to love them or come to hate them."

"And that's what your life is always about? Discovering who can be trusted and who can't?"

"Sometimes. Often you already know who you can trust, and it's all about figuring out how much not to trust everyone else."

"How much not to trust?"

She got up on one elbow so she could look at his face. "Jimmy, everyone has limits. Certain limits are fixed. Certain limits are flexible. It just depends on the individual. For example, I bet you couldn't think of a situation where you would steal. I'm not talking about taking bread to avoid starvation or to feed a hungry child, I'm talking about theft for gain."

"So where are my limits flexible?"

"Your wife was the love of your life. You never cheated on her, right?"

He nodded.

"She died very quickly from a horrible cancer. It devastated you. You'd want the world to know that. And yet..." She leaned down and kissed him. "Two months later we've hiding the fact that we're sleeping together from your kids."

"It doesn't seem like a contradiction to me. Stacey would understand. Besides, we aren't hiding. Bell sort of asked, and I sort of told her. We're just being respectful of their feelings."

"Just being respectful of their feelings?"

"We give them a little more time, then everything comes out in the open."

"It's going to be more difficult than you think."

"I know my kids."

"Bell gave me the talk."

"What?"

"When you were golfing. Told me she and her brother had their eyes on me. Didn't trust me. Were afraid I was taking advantage of you, even if they couldn't figure out how."

"I'll talk to her."

"Please don't. She'll just think the problem is even worse than she thought."

"Oh, Nicki." He pulled her close. "You've got nothing to worry about. I want you to stay as long as you want to stay. I hope John never needs your help."

AT THE GOLDMINER'S CLUB, Rudy Grissom, Kevin Johnson, and Chris Billings, all dressed in black pants and black T-shirts, moved about the dimly lit room, keeping an eye on the customers. Up on the stage a blonde wearing only a black cowgirl hat gyrated to an upbeat country song about horses, ranching, and true love. Women in lingerie with toy pistols strapped to their hips moved about the room serving drinks and soliciting private dances. Three men sat at the seats along the stage, ogling the dancer—a bearded man, a tall man wearing glasses, and a bald man with a fringe of blond hair. They were all drunk. The bearded one leaned across the stage and grabbed the dancer by the ankle. Billings and Johnson came at him from both sides and grabbed him by the collar of his sports coat and his arms. The dancer backed up a step and kept dancing. They dragged the bearded drunk to the door and tossed him out into the parking lot as his friends protested and hurried behind.

"You can't touch the dancers," Johnson said.

"We want our cover money back," the tall guy said.

"We spent a lot of money," the bald guy said.

Johnson pushed him away.

"You can't throw me out," the bearded drunk said. He stumbled toward the door.

Billings hopped into the air, cocked back his arm, and swung down with all his force. The drunk hit the pavement with a sickening thud, his nose mashed and blood splattered across his face. His friends stopped in their tracks.

"Christ, what did you do that for?" the tall guy said. "He wasn't swinging on you."

Billings pointed out into the parking lot. "Get out of here."

The bald guy squatted down beside their friend. "Toby, Toby, you all right?" He looked up at Billings. "You knocked him out." He turned to the tall guy. "Hey, Mark, give me a hand."

They picked up Toby by the shoulders and dragged him to their car.

Johnson shook his head. "You could've killed that guy."

"Too bad. He shouldn't have been a prick."

Grissom came up behind them. "All settled?"

"Chris fucked that boy up," Johnson said.

"What did I tell you about using too much force?" Grissom asked.

"He wasn't inside, so nobody saw," Billings said.

"You've got to take it easy with the customers. We don't need any lawsuits."

Billings shrugged.

"I'm not kidding. You've got to settle down."

"Asshole got what he had coming. He shouldn't have touched the dancer."

Grissom went back inside. Billings turned to Johnson. "You see the way that dude's head popped off the pavement?"

"You're a fucking monster."

"Got that right."

"Need to chain you up."

"Assholes better be afraid of me."

3

THE SAFE-DEPOSIT BOX

C had sat in a stolen Ford Fiesta on the street across from Robertson's law office. He'd been sitting here every day since he arrived in town, studying the movements of the lawyer, the secretary, and Molly. She was an excellent liar, but she couldn't lie to him. He could see right through her. Something had happened in the month since they had split up to outrun the detectives—something more than just her learning a new con. Her loyalties were shifting. Why else would she refuse to rip off the lawyer and get out of town when he told her the detective had been at his motel?

He watched the lawyer come out of the office and get into his blue BMW. He glanced at his watch. Five p.m. Never varied. Molly would be next, followed by the secretary. The door would be locked by 5:30. Opened at 9:00 a.m. Lunch from noon to 1:00. Secretary always left exactly at noon. Molly at 12:20. She was probably screwing Robertson in his office. And he knew she was screwing John. He'd seen them together, seen the way she hung on his every word. Well, he wasn't going to let the old grifter keep her. She was his. She was going to leave with him. He lit a cigarette. He just had to give her a little push.

JOHN WAS SITTING by himself in a booth at Irish Eyes, a bar in a strip mall near his apartment. Happy hour was in full swing. The place was jammed with drinkers angling for an open stool or table. The bartenders, wearing white shirts with the sleeves rolled up and green suspenders, were working like machines on an assembly line. John scanned the crowd while he sipped his beer. No one in the bar for him to be concerned about. He took out his phone and speed-dialed Nicole. "Is this a good time?"

"Just a sec. I'm walking out onto the deck." There was a pause. "What's up?"

"Just wanted to chat."

"How's that job going? Do you need me?"

"Don't worry yourself. This little scheme is beneath your abilities. The new girl is working out just fine."

"Just fine? I see. You fucking her?"

"Of course I'm fucking her. I'm doing everything I got to do to keep the pieces moving around the board. I'm her boyfriend, her dad, and her brother—whatever I need to be at any given moment." Silence. "You jealous?"

"I'm not jealous."

"You're jealous. Why? You've got nothing to worry about."

"Because she's there with you, doing our thing. Cuddling in our bed. Am I supposed to like that?"

"But you're there with Denison."

"I'm not fucking him in our bed."

John smiled. "You know how crazy that sounds, don't you?"

"You're not charming your way out of this."

He sipped his beer. "Denison's daughter giving you a bad time?"

"She's been a little bitchy, but I think it's mainly her way of being loyal to her mother."

"Well, the new kid isn't going to replace you, so relax. Remember when we were first working together? You were a natural. Her skill level is not even in your ballpark. Focus on winning over the daughter—what's her name?"

"Bell."

"Win her over. As soon as she's your best buddy, the son doesn't stand a chance. Then your days of heavy lifting will be over. Who knows? Denison might even marry you."

"What makes you think I want to marry him?"

"Baby, you know you want out of the game."

"I don't want out."

"But how many times have you told me that you think you're getting too old to seduce the marks? Come on, there's only two outcomes here. One, you ride off into the sunset with Denison, a guy you care a great deal about—hell, you might even love him someday —or two, we make some gigantic score so that we never have to work again. Which is more likely? That's all I'm saying. Take the retirement package and make the best of it. Don't worry about our relationship. I'll always have your back."

The line was quiet for a moment.

"We're not done talking about this, but I'm going to change the subject," Nicole said. "Remember that idiot who was stealing credit card numbers at the Save-U-Mart? It was, like, five years ago. I ran into him the day before yesterday."

"That's a strange coincidence. You know how I feel about those. Have you got a gun?"

"A gun? Please. That guy couldn't walk and chew gum. I talked him down."

"Good for you. Now go out and get a gun. Something that fits in your purse and feels comfortable in your hand. Maybe Denison has one he hasn't told you about."

"I don't want any of our connections around James."

"Go to a gun store. A legit gun is better than no gun at all."

"You're so sweet when you worry about me. I wish I was sitting in your lap right now with my arms around your neck."

"Did Denison and his daughter find out?"

"They were with me."

"How did they take it?"

"I told them the truth, more or less. James knows who we are, so he just shrugged it off. And I think Bell is finally beginning to understand why me and her dad are so close."

"So you worked it to your advantage."

"James asked me to go to California with him."

"Excellent. When you going?"

"At the end of the month. He needs to be out there to help with his homeless women program."

"I thought he was already dealing with that one-on-one."

"I'm not homeless. I could always wash up on your doorstep."

"I might not open the door. But seriously, get a gun."

"Love you too."

LATER THAT EVENING, after supper, Bell stood out on the beach talking to her brother on the phone. Even though the sun was falling in the west, windsurfers still sailed back and forth in the near distance, and gulls still circled above, ready to swoop down on anything that might be edible.

She kicked at the sand. "Skip, I'm working at it. It's going to be a lot harder than we thought. You're not going to believe what happened the first night I was here." She filled him in.

"So she's a professional swindler," Skip said. "Somebody who she put in jail confronted her. And she and Dad became friends after she helped him in Nohamay City. Jesus Christ."

"Yeah. I put her on notice yesterday. Told her we had our eyes on her."

"What did she say?"

"In so many words? That she loved Dad and wouldn't do anything to hurt him."

"Like you could believe her."

"I'm telling you, Skip, she's charming and helpful. And you've got to admit Dad's been doing better since she arrived."

"Are they in the same bedroom?"

"They were before I got here. Now she has her own room, but they must be sleeping together. They're very discreet."

"Is he crushing on her?"

"No, he's not fawning; he's like his regular self."

"So there's no end in sight?"

"Your guess is as good as mine," Bell said. "I've got to go home in a little over two weeks. I'm teaching a new class this fall, and I haven't started planning it yet."

"I know you're doing your best. I appreciate you taking the lead on this. If I can move enough appointments, maybe I can come out to help."

"I don't know if it will do any good. We might just have to wait this thing out."

"I'm not saying it's the same thing, but I'm a little concerned that Dad is taking his magical thinking a little too far."

"What do you mean?"

"Look, none of us wanted Mom to die, but we had to accept reality. Dad wouldn't even have been in Nohamay City if he hadn't been unwilling to accept the facts. How much did he pay that hospital to use Mom as a pincushion? And this is the same thing. He doesn't really know this woman, but he thinks he's in love with her. We should give him some more time, but maybe in six months or so, if his thinking doesn't sharpen up, we should talk him into a brain scan to make sure he didn't have a brain bleed or something from all the pressure he was under during Mom's cancer."

"You think there might be something physically wrong with Dad?"

"I don't know. All I'm saying is that his behavior now is different than before Mom got sick. You know it. I know it. That's why you're down there, and we're on the phone talking like conspirators."

"I don't like going behind his back."

"Me, neither, but he's our dad. If we're got to protect him from himself, that's what we've got to do.

THE NEXT DAY, as soon as Betty left for lunch, Molly headed for Robertson's private office. She was wearing a tapestry-print shirtdress and no panties. She unbuttoned the top two buttons of the dress. It was only the third day of their relationship, but when he put his hands on her, she knew that she was completely in control. It was almost pathetic, the ease with which she could use her body to manipulate him. And sober, it was so much easier to read his tells. Today she was going to try out her pouty voice and see if she could make him come even quicker. When she stepped into his office, he was on the phone.

He held up a finger. "Got you. I'll be expecting him." He hung up. "Have a seat."

"What's up, Neal?"

"I've got to change my plans. I need you to go to the bank for me. You got a problem carrying cash?"

"Not in broad daylight."

He reached into a drawer of his desk and took out a fat manila envelope and a key. "Are you familiar with safe-deposit boxes?"

She shook her head.

"Here's the sealed envelope and the safe-deposit-box key. Be sure you're carrying a photo ID. At Milton Bank, they'll have you sign the access ledger and check your ID signature against the ledger signature. Then they'll use your key and their key to open the box, which they take into a private room for you. You put the envelope in the box. Then you take the box back the teller, and she puts it away and gives your key back."

"That sounds simple enough."

"This is the important part. This safe-deposit box belongs to a very special client. Do not touch anything in the box. Understand?"

"Yes."

"The client knows exactly what's in there. If anything is missing, he'll know."

"You can count on me."

"If there's a problem, I won't cover for you."

"There won't be any problems."

"Great."

Robertson picked up his desk phone and speed-dialed the Milton Bank manager's private line. "Walter? It's Neal. I've got a new assistant. I want you to put her on the safe-deposit-box list. I'll email the specifics right now."

He hung up the phone. "That's that. Come see me when you get back."

Molly rebuttoned her dress as she headed out to her car. She had the key. How much money could possibly be in the safe-deposit box? $25,000? $50,000? Her work was finally going to pay off. As soon as she was out of sight of the office, she called John. "He gave me the safe-deposit-box key. I'm going to the bank."

"Excellent."

"Are you meeting me there?"

"Let's not get ahead of ourselves. What did he tell you to do?"

She reported what Robertson had said.

"So he's expecting you back in a few minutes. You disappear now, you won't make it to the state line. Once the bank has you in its records, you can get in the safe-deposit box anytime. We'll give it a couple of days and then steal the key. That way we'll have plenty of time to disappear before they find out the money is gone. Okay?"

"Okay."

Traffic was heavy in the downtown business zone, with drivers honking their horns or yelling at jaywalkers. The crosswalks were full of people on their lunch breaks. Traffic stopped in her lane where a tow truck was loading a banged-up white truck. Molly nosed her way into the other lane. So they weren't taking the money today. That meant she still had time to decide. Was she going to leave with John —partner with him, learn the long con, make the kind of money she'd only dreamed of? Or was she going to stay with Chad? They had history. She knew she could count on him. But what was loyalty worth, compared to taking the next step? With Chad, they were always on the short con, hustling marks for their pocket money, emptying cash registers, forging checks, or using stolen credit cards.

That was never going to change. If she wanted to move on, now was the time.

Milton Bank was on her right. She pulled into the bank's parking lot and parked nearest the doors. But John owed her nothing. She couldn't trust him. If a more experienced girl came along, she'd be out. Right now she had all the power because she was the only one who could get into the safe-deposit box. But maybe she didn't need a man. Manipulating Robertson had been easy enough. If she stole the key by herself, she could take all the cash, and leave both John and Chad behind. She was the one who did all the work. Why did she always have to give half the money to a man?

LATER THAT AFTERNOON in Cricket Bay, Stein sat in his car in the parking lot of the Shoot-the-Moon mini-golf watching Sally, Denison, and the redhead making their way around the course. He'd been following them for two days, morning to night, and he still had no idea what Sally's scheme was. They went shopping. They went to restaurants. They hung out on the beach. Sally never went anywhere by herself. Were she and the redhead ripping off Denison? Was she ripping off the redhead and Denison? It had to be one or the other; Denison had too much money to be involved in some crooked scheme. They were at hole number seven, the giant clown head, laughing and gesturing as if they were having a grand time.

What was Sally's game? There had to be some way to figure out what she was up to. She owed him $60,000. He had to have that money. It would keep his family from being put out on the street. He'd told Carrie that the imaginary interview had gone fine and that he had to stay in town for the second interview. He only had a day or two more before he'd have to tell her something else. They moved on to hole number eight. There was no reason to continue sitting here. Maybe he could learn something new online.

"Sorry I didn't call yesterday. I was swamped with grading," Bobby said.

Bell sat at the umbrella table on the deck at the beach house, looking out over the darkening sea. The wind was up, and even though it was almost twilight, a man was out on the beach flying a kite. "That's okay, honey. It was just another day in paradise."

"That bad?"

"Nicole somehow manages to treat me like I'm her sister and like she's just a visitor. And Dad seems more and more like his old self."

"Good news, but not what you hoped for."

"Hearing Dad on the phone was just a lot different from actually being here."

"Yeah, I know how that goes. So you're beginning to like her?"

"I wouldn't go that far. I'm still not convinced she's going to be good for Dad in the long run. I just think her involvement with him is more innocent than I originally thought."

"Have you talked to your brother?"

"He's major pissed. Of course, he's not here. I tried to explain, but he thinks maybe Dad's behavior is caused be a brain bleed or something from all the stress of Mom's cancer."

"I don't know, honey. All of you have been through a heavy emotional time. That can cause people to act different."

"I know." She got out a handkerchief and dabbed at her eyes. "It's all just so raw. And there Dad is, smiling, holding her hand. When I think of her fucking him, I want to choke her."

"You need a hug."

"You think? Almost bought a pack of cigarettes yesterday."

"You should tell your dad that we're getting married."

"It's too soon."

"We don't have to get married right away. We can wait 'til next spring, but he deserves to know. Skip too. They deserve to be happy for you."

"I'll think about it."

"Good." He paused for a moment. "Since there's nothing else you can do there, why don't you come home early?"

"I'd love to. But this is the last chance I get to be with Dad for a while. And I don't want to listen to Skip bitch about it. So it's just the usual dysfunctional family bullshit. Those are my excuses, and I'm sticking to them."

"Try to get a good night's sleep."

"I love you."

"I love you."

4

MOLLY'S PLAN

The next morning, while Molly was driving to work, the money in the safe-deposit box at Milton Bank kept popping up in her mind. Fat envelopes stacked in the box. The envelopes she's peeked in had been full of hundred-dollar bills, so there had to be well over $100,000 in the box. That was real money. The kind of money that belonged to dangerous criminals. John must know who they are. His connection would have told him. And yet he wasn't the least bit worried about stealing from them.

She turned onto Thackeray Drive. But why should he be? No one had seen him. He wasn't working in Neal's office. No, if they came for anyone, it would be her. Was John's escape plan good enough to protect her? Or was it just good enough to protect him? She pulled into the parking lot of Robertson's law office and parked away from the door. She was taking all the risk, but she was only getting half the money, and that was after the 10 percent they paid to the connection. If he existed at all.

She'd made up her mind. If she could get the safe-deposit-box key herself, she'd take all the money and stiff John. If she couldn't, she'd stick with John. Chad was out of the picture. It was time for her to move on.

Robertson was at the courthouse that morning. After Betty left for lunch, Molly saw her chance. She slipped into Robertson's private office, leaving the door slightly ajar. She glanced around the room. When he'd sent her to the bank, he'd taken the key from the middle top drawer of his desk, so she started there. No luck—just the usual assortment of pens, Post-it notes, and paperclips. The top right drawer held a Colt .357 and a box of shells. The gun seemed out of character. Neal was a talker, not a fighter. The middle drawer contained a set of headphones, an old iPhone, and a pint of Jim Beam. Now that was the Neal Robertson she knew. The bottom drawer was files of open cases. Where could the key be? There weren't any other drawers in the room. Just then, she heard the front door open. She stepped from behind the desk. Robertson came into the office with his briefcase in one hand. "What're you doing?"

"Looking for the Stevens divorce file. I need to make copies. I thought it might be on your desk."

He set his briefcase down on his desktop. "I don't think it's here."

"Must have missed it in the copier room."

She turned to go. He caught her by the wrist. "What's your hurry?"

"No hurry." She kissed him.

He ran his hands over her ass.

"Betty won't back for another thirty minutes," she said.

He smiled. She bent over the desk and hiked up her skirt.

"You're making me crazy."

"You telling me you don't love it?"

He dropped his pants. Just then, the door crashed open, and Chad charged into the office, pointing and yelling. "Get off her, asshole! You're not using my sister for a whore! Your wife is going to hear about this!"

"Get out of here," Molly yelled. She tried to get up, but Robertson pushed her back down on the desk.

Robertson looked straight at Chad. "What kind of idiot are you? I'll do whatever I want. You can't blackmail me." He smacked Molly's rump. "You going to stay and watch? Get the fuck out of here."

Chad rushed around the desk and grabbed Robertson by the front of his shirt, pushing him back to the wall. Molly squeezed out of the way. "Stop it," she yelled. "Stop it."

Robertson's feet were tangled in his pants. Chad punched him in the face. Robertson threw up his arms and then clawed at Chad's face. Chad lurched backward. Robertson fell forward onto his desk, jerked the top drawer open, and pulled out the Colt. As he turned toward Chad, Chad dived at him, both hands grabbing for the gun.

"No! No!" Molly yelled.

The gun went off, the sound banging around the room. Chad crumpled to the floor, grabbing at Robertson as he fell. Robertson fired again. Then he turned and looked at Molly, the .357 hanging loose in his hand. She breathed in hard, as if she were going to scream, spun on her heels, and ran.

Robertson set the gun down on his desk. "Fuck. Fuck. Fuck." He pulled up his pants, reached into the second drawer of his desk for the Jim Beam, and took a slug from the bottle. Then he stepped over to Chad and poked him with his shoe. Dead.

He walked over to the open door, looked out into the reception area to make sure it was empty, closed the door, and went back to his desk and sat down. Think. Take a breath. This couldn't have been an accident. Molly and this guy must have been in it together. He looked over at the body. Blood was already pooling on the carpet. He couldn't clean this up by himself. He took another slug of bourbon. There was only one thing he could do. He didn't want to, but it was all that was left. He couldn't risk making things worse than they already were. He took out his throwaway cell phone.

"Spanish? It's Neal. I made a mistake. I need your help."

"What phone are you using?" Spanish Mike asked.

"The throwaway."

"Don't say anything else. Where are you?"

"I'm at my office."

"I'm sending some guys right over."

John was back in Irish Eyes, sitting at the bar, sipping a cup of black coffee. The place was almost empty. The bartender was on his knees behind the bar, restocking the soft drink refrigerator. Three retired guys were sitting at a table in the corner playing rummy and nursing their beers. John had just come from Mail N More, where he'd visited his rented locker and left a manila envelope containing their escape packet: new IDs, credit cards, and $5000 cash. All the details were now in place. All they had to do was steal the safe-deposit-box key, take the money, collect their new identities, and disappear. He still hadn't quite decided if he should bring Molly with him or cut her loose. He was going to have to make up his mind. If he brought her along, Nicole would be furious. He'd have to set some strict boundaries on his relationship with Molly—no more sex, for starters—and that might make it difficult to keep her in line. But it couldn't be helped. Sex with partners was different than sex with civilians. It created jealousy, hierarchies of intimacy and loyalty. No, inside their crew, he and Nicole had to be alpha, and there couldn't be any confusion about that. If Nicole was going to continue seeing Denison, he needed a reliable partner. Someone trainable. He just couldn't find a new person for every job. So he was just going to have to suck it up and win Nicole over to his plan. His smartphone rang. It was Molly.

"Yeah?"

"John," She sounded as if she were crying. "It's all gone to hell. Neal shot Chad."

John stood up and walked away from the bar. "Slow down. Where are you?"

"I'm in my car in the QuikSnack parking lot."

"Okay. Neal shot Chad?"

"I ran."

"Take a breath. Who's Chad?"

"The guy you saw me with."

John sat down at a table. "Start at the beginning. Don't leave anything out."

Molly explained what happened.

"I told you to wait, but you couldn't. So right after you got access to the safe-deposit box, you blew the job up. All that money lost. I didn't believe that guy at the coffee shop was an old boyfriend, but I didn't think you were a fool."

"Hey, I didn't know he was going to barge in there. I didn't have anything to do with that."

"It's a little late for woulda, coulda, shoulda."

"I'll make it right. I'll do whatever you say. I'll go back in there and tell him I panicked."

John thought for a minute. "No. He's spooked now. Going back is a death sentence. You need to disappear. Don't go to your apartment."

"I can't leave my stuff."

"You've got a credit card and a bank card, don't you? Get out of town."

He put his phone back in his pocket. What a clusterfuck. A month's work wasted. This was exactly the problem he avoided by not working with new partners. If Nicole had been here, they'd be counting the money right now. Well, so much for Molly. What had she been up to? Was it her plan to surprise him by getting the key on her own or was she planning to cheat him? At least he had some distance from this problem. Robertson had never met him. He went back to the bar. The bartender looked toward him. "You want that coffee freshened up?"

"No, thanks," he said. "I've got to go."

MOLLY's small blue suitcase lay open on her unmade bed. She flipped over the dresser drawer of underwear into the suitcase, dropped the drawer onto the bed, and smoothed out the pile of panties with her hands. There was still room for her bras. The large suitcase, already packed, stood by the front door. She looked at her watch. Hard to believe that Chad was alive an hour ago. What an idiot. She was going to miss him. She teared up. She wiped her eyes with the back of her hand. Not now. No time for feelings. She was on her own. She'd screwed up, and John had dropped her. She needed to keep moving. She pushed the bras into the suitcase and closed it. As she wheeled the suitcase to the front door, she glanced around the apartment for anything that she couldn't leave behind. All packed. She wheeled the suitcases, one in each hand, toward the elevator. Then she changed her mind, pushed through the door to the stairwell, and stopped. She heard the elevator open and heavy footsteps start down the hall.

She picked up her suitcases just as someone started pounding on a door. "Ms. Wright! Ms. Wright!" She set the suitcases down and ran down three flights of stairs and out the fire exit into the sunny parking lot. Two clean-cut Latino men wearing charcoal suits were waiting by a black Avalon parked next to her car. She veered toward the street. The taller one, who had a knife tattoo on his neck, caught her by the arm before she reached the sidewalk.

"Don't struggle. It'll only make things painful." He led her back to the Avalon and pushed her into the back seat. "Carlos," he said, "look up the stairs and make sure she didn't leave anything behind."

A few minutes later, Carlos came out of the stairwell with her suitcases in his hands. "That's all of it. Frankie and Lu are in the apartment."

"Let's go." Knife Tattoo got in the backseat with Molly.

They drove downtown into the old industrial zone by the railroad tracks. Molly sat very still, Knife Tattoo's hard fingers tight around her wrist. She wanted to say something, anything, but she didn't know any words that could help. John told her to keep Chad out of it, but she hadn't, and he'd blindsided her. John told her not to go back to the apartment, but she had to have her clothes. Now she wasn't sure she was going to leave with her life. She tried to control her breathing. What did they really know? A guy claiming to be her brother had threatened Neal, gotten into a fight, gotten shot. She was a witness. Was that the worst of it?

They pulled up to a rusted sheet-metal building adjacent to the tracks. Carlos honked the horn. A garage door went up. They drove in and stopped near an old school teacher's desk. Two men in janitor's uniforms lowered the door behind them. Knife Tattoo pulled her out of the car.

A small, thin Latino man wearing a black suit with an open-collared black shirt stood up from the teacher's chair. "This her? Robertson's girl?"

"Yeah, Spanish," Knife Tattoo said. "It's her. She was about to skip when we caught her. We got her bags in the car."

"Carlos," Spanish said, "go through those bags." He turned to Molly. "Have a seat, my dear."

Knife Tattoo pushed her down into a folding chair facing the desk. Spanish clasped his hands behind his back. "Do you know who I am?"

Molly shook her head.

"I'm Spanish Mike. I'm a business partner of Neal's. When your—what are we calling him? Your brother? When he ended up dead, Neal called me. Asked me to clean up his mess. That's what I'm doing. Cleaning up the mess. Are you part of the mess?"

"No," Molly said. "No, I'm not. I ran because I was afraid."

Spanish nodded sympathetically. "Of course you were afraid. Who wouldn't be? Who were you afraid of? Neal? The dead guy? The police?"

"I was just scared. The fight. The gunshots. I panicked."

"Sure. You were scared. But why were you leaving town?"

"I didn't want to be involved. I like Neal. I didn't want to have to testify."

"So you were trying to be helpful? You were afraid he would be arrested?"

She nodded. "Yes, that's exactly it."

"Somehow," he said, "I don't believe you."

Molly looked from Spanish Mike to Knife Tattoo and back again. She looked down at her hands. She hadn't realized she was trembling. She wanted so badly to wake up, to go get a drink of water, to go back to bed, but she knew this wasn't a dream.

"Let's start with the guy. Who is he?"

Molly opened her mouth to speak, but no sound came out.

"Look. You're connected with Neal. You're one of his people. If you haven't done anything too bad—if you've just made a stupid mistake

—you don't have to die. You just get your wrist slapped, go on probation."

"That guy was my ex."

"That wasn't so hard, was it?"

"He came into town, started threatening me. I didn't want to say anything to Neal because I thought he might fire me to avoid the drama."

"Why did he say he was your brother?"

"Did he? Everything is a blur. I don't know exactly what happened."

"How much money were you hoping to get from Neal?"

"What? Money?" She shook her head. "I don't know what you're talking about."

Spanish Mike lit a cigarette. "Who's your partner?"

"I don't have a partner. I didn't have anything going with Chad."

"Do you smoke?"

She shook her head.

"I know your ex wasn't your partner. But who is? You just didn't wash up at Neal's office."

"I don't have a partner."

"You ever been in a bad relationship? You ever love a man who beat you? A man who burned you with cigarettes?"

Knife Tattoo stepped behind her and pressed down on her shoulders. Spanish Mike continued. "Hurts like hell the first time."

He took a hit off the cigarette and lowered the lit end to her face just below her left eye. She pulled her head back as far as she could. He chuckled. "You're going to tell me before we're done."

"John," she blurted out. "John Ferguson."

"That sounds like the truth." Spanish Mike dropped the cigarette and stepped on it. "You feel better already, don't you? Getting that secret off your chest. Want something to drink?" He turned to Knife Tattoo. "Go get her a Coca-Cola."

LATER, when it was just dark enough for the streetlights to come on,

John came out of his apartment with his car keys in his hand. He was all packed. The apartment was completely clean. There was nothing in there to tie him to this place. One stop at the Mail N More to pick up his escape packet, and he would be on his way. It would be as if he'd never been there. When he reached his Cadillac, two Latino men in dark suits got out of the black Avalon parked across from him.

"Ferguson."

John turned.

"Keep your hands in the open," the taller one said. The shorter one held an automatic pistol down at his side.

John watched them, sizing them up, waiting to see if the taller one would get in the way of the shorter one's line of fire, giving him the opportunity to draw his Glock, but he didn't.

The taller one smiled. "You know a girl named Molly Wright?"

John shook his head. "No. What's this about? Who are you guys?"

"You're coming with us."

"No, I'm not."

"You're going to answer some questions. If you got the right answers, you'll be on your way."

"Sorry, but I'm getting in my car."

The shorter one pushed the barrel of his pistol into John's side. "You want to get shot?"

The taller one took John's Glock out of his side holster. John held his hands up in surrender. They put John in the front seat passenger's side of the Avalon. The taller man drove and the shorter man sat behind John with the pistol pointed at John's neck.

"Where are we going?" John asked.

"Shut up," the taller man said.

They drove across town to a group of ramshackle warehouses and pulled up to an old sheet-metal building. It looked like the kind of place where questions got asked and answered. Molly must have been too slow leaving town. The garage door rose, and they rolled inside.

"Get out," the taller man said.

In the light, John could see a knife tattoo on the man's neck. The two men pushed John toward a folding chair in front of an old school teacher's desk. Molly was nowhere in sight. A small, thin Latino man wearing a black suit sat drinking a Coca-Cola with his feet up on the desk. "Do you know who I am?"

John nodded. Spanish Mike. This was as bad as it got. Pleading ignorance was only going to lead to a beating. How could he massage the facts? What had Molly told them?

"Have we ever met?"

"No, sir."

"But you know me?"

"By reputation. Yes, sir."

"Sit down."

John sat on the folding chair.

"Do you know Molly Wright?"

John nodded. "Sir, if I had known that Robertson belonged to you I wouldn't have gone after him. That would have been an amazingly stupid thing to do."

"You got that right."

"And I had nothing to do with the boyfriend or whoever the hell he was. That was a bonehead play."

"Yes it was. Left quite a mess to clean up." Spanish Mike stood up. "So why were you going after Robertson?"

"Honestly? He's a putz. He was meant to be conned. Come on, the guy might be a decent lawyer, but I'm not telling you anything when I say he thinks way too highly of himself."

Spanish Mike nodded slightly. Knife Tattoo punched John in the side of the head. John careened sideways, and the other man kicked John's chair out from under him. He fell hard on his side. Knife Tattoo kicked him in the stomach.

"I want to believe you," Spanish Mike said. "How much money did you think you would get?"

John clutched his stomach and tried to take in enough air to speak. "How can I make this right? How can I pay you for your inconvenience?"

Knife Tattoo kicked him in the kidney.

"Twenty grand," John said. "Heard he was good for twenty grand."

"That's enough," Spanish Mike said. "Put him with the girl."

IN CRICKET BAY, Stein sat in his car in the dark, watching Denison's house. Over the last three days he'd learned nothing from following them or researching them online. They all seemed to be following the kind of routine that normal, innocent people followed. They didn't even go out clubbing at night. A bank of clouds drifted across the moon. How much longer could things go on like this? The summer season was winding down fast. All the rich vacationers were leaving town. When would his window of opportunity close? He got out his phone and called Grissom. "Hey."

"What's up?"

"You got the guys?"

"I've got them lined up."

"What did you tell them we were doing?"

"Trying to get some money back."

"And these guys will do it for the five grand?"

"I think so. Have you figured out her scam?"

"Not yet. I'm worried we're going to miss our chance if we don't get moving."

"We can't highjack their scam if we don't know what it is."

"So far she looks completely clean."

"But her boyfriend has the money."

"Absolutely. I checked him out online."

"It's probably going to be his money anyway, isn't it?"

"What are you saying?"

"If she's scamming the boyfriend, and we're going to rob her, we're taking the boyfriend's money."

"That's one way to look at it."

"So why not do a home invasion? Boom, we got the money. You don't have to figure anything out."

"I don't know, Rudy, that seems...I'm not ready for that."

"Okay, Fred, it's your plan. Get in touch when you've decided what you're going to do."

Stein watched the shadows through the windows of Denison's house. What was he doing here? Getting his money back—even his money back with extra to pay Rudy and some guys, seemed a lot different than robbing Denison. He didn't know the guy. And Denison hadn't done anything to him. As far as he could tell, Denison was just the chump du jour, just like he'd been. But Rudy was right, his plan had been to take Sally's money as soon as she stole it, not give it back to Denison or whoever the chump turned out to be. So how was robbing Denison any different? Denison would still just be paying for being stupid enough to get involved with Sally.

Stein started his car. They weren't going anywhere tonight. He might as well go back to the motel. Time was running out. Home invasion? He was going to have to make a decision.

JOHN, Molly, and Chad were crammed together in the trunk of the Avalon as it bounced along what was probably a dirt road. John's and Molly's wrists were cuffed behind their backs with disposable plastic handcuffs. Chad stank of day-old diaper and dry blood. Molly was whimpering. Her tears were soaking into the shoulder of John's shirt. She whispered, "Sorry I gave you up. I knew it wouldn't do any good. But when he held the lit cigarette up to my cheek..."

"Not dead yet. You tell them anything about the job?"

"They didn't even ask. They think it was just a shakedown gone wrong."

"So this is just the cleanup from the shooting. I didn't realize Robertson was that important to them."

The car hit a pothole. Chad's head bumped against the side of Molly's face, and she began to sob. It seemed as if they were traveling uphill. John tried to focus his mind. Molly was weaker than used dishwater. She'd be no help at all. He already knew that the cuffs were too tight to slip out of. When should he start running? As soon as he stepped out of the trunk? No, both of them would have their guns drawn then. He'd have to judge moment by moment. One thing was certain. They didn't want to carry him to the hole. If these guys were any good at this, the grave would be off the road down some well-used animal trail, which would give him more opportunity to make a break for it. The car slowed to a stop. The doors opened and shut. John heard talking, but he couldn't make out what they were saying. The trunk popped open. In the moonlight he could see tall pine trees on both sides of the narrow road.

"Get up out of there."

John sat up. Somebody grabbed him by his shoulders and pulled him out of the trunk. As soon as his feet hit the ground, this guy shoved him around to the side of the car and pushed the barrel of a pistol into his ribs. In the Avalon's headlights he saw another car, a sedan, and a grave dug in front of it right in the middle of the road.

Another guy pulled Molly from the trunk. She lost her footing and fell in a heap. "Get up," the man said.

He half dragged Molly over next to John. She saw the grave, gasped, and fell to her knees. John was trying to get his bearings. There were four guys, all armed—the two that brought them and the two that dug the hole. They were in the woods on a ridge, probably in Coon River State Park. The ground fell sharply away maybe ten feet to his right. When the wind shifted, he could faintly hear moving water. The two guys who had brought them there lugged Chad out of the trunk and carried him up the hill past the other car, whining about his smell and his weight as they shuffled along. When they got to the hole, they gave him a strong swing and tossed him in.

"Come on, sister." The guy who had Molly's arm pulled her to her feet.

"No," she said. "No. You don't have to do this."

"Yeah? Don't make this hurt any more than it has to."

Molly dug her heels into the dirt and dropped to the ground. The guy dragged her toward the hole. The two guys who were standing there started laughing.

"Give me a hand, assholes."

"Shoot her already. Dragging her alive or dragging her dead—it's the same thing."

One of the guys by the grave picked up a shovel, walked over to Molly, and whacked her across the shoulders. "Get up."

"How is that helping? Grab her other arm."

Molly's skirt was twisted around her legs, and the buttons on her blouse had popped off. The guy next to John shifted around to watch the show, the barrel of his pistol slipping away from John's ribs. "Hey, Carlos. You guys fuck her?"

The man with the shovel said, "Why? You want to have a go?"

"We should at least have a look. She's not going anywhere."

Molly screamed as she scrambled up off the ground. She head-butted the first guy just before Carlos grabbed her arm. John kicked his guy in the knee and ran for the drop off. He heard two shots, but that just made him run faster. He dove off the side of the hill, crashing through the brush, his arms tied behind his back, branches jabbing through his clothes and tall grass stinging his face. A rotten section of tree trunk at the edge of the water knocked the wind out of him. He saw stars.

He sucked in air and tried to be still. He could hear the men moving above him, near the road, cursing and blaming one another as they started down the hill. Flashlight beams. He couldn't stay here. He crawled over the tree trunk and fell into the running water. When he found his footing, the water came up to his shoulders. To his right was a hollow in the bank that had been carved out by the current. He walked three steps and leaned into the heavy roots of an old tree under the bank. He was cold and hungry and angry. He had a sharp pain in his side. His wrists hurt where the plastic cuffs cut into them. He strained to hear the guys climbing down the hill, but all he could hear was running water. He dug his feet into the creek bed and waited. Finally he heard the crunching of weeds and then nearby voices.

"He must have gone in the water."

"We can't know for sure."

"He didn't run out of here. Frankie and Lu are blocking the path and we've been all through these weeds."

"How deep is it?"

John saw the flashlight beam move over the water near the place he went in. He stood completely still.

"Deep enough. Asshole must have drowned."

"Then he'll wash up downstream."

"Time's wasting. Let's bury the two we got and get out of here."

The voices grew faint. He was going to have to wait them out. All four of them at it, they'd have the hole filled inside thirty minutes. They wouldn't come back down here. Guys like those lacked patience, and the night was his friend. His stomach rolled over. He felt powerfully thirsty. It was a shame about Molly. She was a stupid kid—she thought she could stiff him and get away on her own—but she didn't deserve to die like that. Fucking Robertson. He was a dead man.

A FEW HOURS later John came out of the creek at a shallow place where a sandbar ran down from a pasture protected by a barbed-wire fence. The moon was high. He could see a section of road on the other side of the pasture. As he walked through a broken place in the fence, he noticed a strand of barbed wire that was at the right height and ran his handcuffs back and forth over it until the cuffs snapped. He looked at his wrists. Not too much damage overall, but the left wrist was dripping blood. He tore a strip of cloth from his shirttail and wrapped the wrist. He pulled up his shirt. There was a gash running along his ribs. He looked at the sky and then at the road beyond the pasture. Which way should he go?

He was walking along the shoulder of the road when he saw headlights. Time to take a chance. He stuck out his thumb. As the headlights neared, they slowed. They belonged to an old Dodge truck driven by an even older man in overalls and a Pioneer Seed cap. He rolled down his window.

"My God, you're a mess."

"Yes, sir."

"You been in an accident? Your car in the ditch around here?"

"No, sir."

"No, sir?"

"It's a long story. Can you give me a ride into town?"

"You ain't killed nobody, have you?"

"No, sir."

The old man tapped his lips with a finger and looked John up and down. "You'll have to ride in the bed. I don't want to get my seats wet."

"Thank you."

John lay on his back in the bed of the truck and rested his head on his folded arms. He was safe now. The old man was a wild card. No one could expect it or plan for it, just like Molly fighting back. Who knew that she was more afraid of being raped than murdered? If she had acted the way it appeared she was going to act, she would have passively gone to her death. And he probably would have joined her. But her boyfriend Chad—was he a wild card, or was he a fuck-up she should have had under control? He'd probably never know now. What he did know was that he couldn't make any more mistakes. Good thing they hadn't taken his shoes. The two one-hundred-dollar bills under the left insole would have to carry him until he could get to his escape packet.

Robertson, looking gray and old, sat at a card table in the back room of Wanda's Whiskey Drop. Cases of beer were stacked against one wall. By the back door, a janitor's mop and bucket leaned up against the side of the electrical box. Spanish Mike sat across from Robertson, two fingers of whiskey in the glass in front of him.

Frankie, the guy who shot Molly, stood facing them.

"So that's your story?"

"Spanish, I'm telling you. I don't know how it happened. But he went into the water with his hands cuffed behind his back. We searched all over. He's got to be dead."

"I see a body; I'll believe he's dead. Get on it."

Frankie opened his mouth to object, thought better of it, and left.

Spanish Mike looked at Robertson. "You can go home now. Your problem is cleaned up. The guy who went in the river?"

Robertson nodded.

"He's a professional grifter. So there had to be more to it than that little money run they tried to pull on you. He had to be working a play. And if he was working a play on you, that means he was working a play on me." Spanish Mike shook his head slowly. "I thought you were a careful guy."

"I am careful, Spanish. I never met this guy. I only ever saw the girl, and she didn't know anything. I promise—"

Spanish Mike pointed at Robertson's chest. "I'm not interested in your promises. You got to own your mistake."

"I understand."

"Do you?"

"Yes."

"Okay then. I'm giving you a pass this time. Nobody gets more than one pass. Is that clear?"

"Yes."

"Get out of here. Give my regards to the missus."

Roberson's chair scraped the floor as he got to his feet. He put his hands into his pockets so that Spanish Mike wouldn't be able to see that they were trembling. What had he done? He'd let his dick get the best of him. He thought no one knew about his relationship with Spanish Mike, but that was obviously wrong if a con man had been after him. He was going to have to lower his profile, stay away from nightclubs and waitresses—at least for the time being. Molly had done this to him—gotten him in trouble with Spanish, put his livelihood at risk—but somehow he still felt sorry for her. He hoped she hadn't suffered. He pushed through the back door and crunched across the gravel parking lot to his car. The darkness seemed like horror-movie darkness, full of terrible possibilities. He wondered if he would ever feel safe again.

JOHN STOOD at the Plexiglas-protected counter of the Sunrise Motel, his clothes muddy and torn, his face scratched, his wrist bandaged. Behind him, two worn-out prostitutes were in negotiations with a tight-fisted truck driver. The big black guy behind the counter eyed him over his gold-framed reading glasses. "Only paying customers here."

John pushed a wet one-hundred-dollar bill through the slot in the Plexiglas. "Need a room." He glanced over his shoulder at the prostitutes. "A quiet room as far from the playground as possible."

The receptionist nodded. "Sure you don't need any refreshment?"

"Already had enough."

"I'm putting you down at the end, away from the ice machine." He pushed the key through the slot. "Checkout is eleven a.m." He counted out two twenties, folded them in half, and slid them through the slot. John picked up his change and the key. The receptionist pointed to the right. John pushed through the smudged glass door out into the parking lot. Two longhaired white guys were selling drugs out of a blue Ford Focus. Another prostitute—white knee-high boots and a skirt not really long enough to hide anything—was leaning into the driver's door of a silver Camry that didn't belong in this neighborhood.

John adjusted his expectations downward with every step he took until he was in his room. Faded drapes smelling heavily of cigarette smoke; a bed with a deep depression in the middle; a stained blanket; towels worn almost a thin as the sheets. He picked up the phone, pressed for an outside line, and called a number he had memorized.

"Terry? I need something in the hundred-dollar range for the complete kit."

"Okey-dokey. Where you at?"

"Sunrise Motel. Room 98."

"You're kidding, right? It's a joke."

"I'm waiting on you. And hurry up. I want to get some sleep before morning."

John sat down on the chair by the door and waited. About thirty minutes later there was a knock. "Yeah?"

"It's me."

John opened the door. A skinny white guy with a missing tooth and bad skin, the pupils of his eyes as big as saucers, was standing in the doorway. "Terry. Great to see you."

John shut the door behind him. Terry went over to the bed and shook a Smith & Wesson revolver out of a wrinkled paper sack. John looked at it hard. "Is it clean?"

"Oh, yeah. Can't claim it's never killed anyone, but it's been wiped, and the numbers have been filed off."

"Looks like a piece of shit."

"It is a piece of shit." He took a baggie of loose ammunition out of his pocket and tossed it down next to the gun.

"I think I'm being taken advantage of."

"It's the middle of the fucking night. If you can wait or you can pay more, it gets better. Afraid it won't shoot? Let's go back in the alley, and you can pop one off." Terry took two throwaway latex gloves out of his pocket and handed them to John. "That's everything."

John handed him a hundred-dollar bill. "Sorry to be so grouchy. It's been a tough day."

"Looks like it."

"Thanks for taking the time."

"You bet. You need anything else, you know where to call."

John locked the door, put on the latex gloves, and loaded the .38. Then he took off the gloves, taking care not to tear them, and used them to handle the gun. He went into the bathroom, laid the gun on the toilet tank, and took a shower. After he toweled off, he looked in the mirror. His chest and back were dotted with bruises and scratches. He was lucky he hadn't lost an eye. He hung his damp clothes over the shower curtain rod, wrapped the extra towel around his waist, and took the .38 back to the bed. He lay down on the bed with the gun laying on the other pillow, hoped there were no bedbugs, and tried to sleep. Spanish Mike's people would be after him as soon as they figured out he wasn't dead. He was a loose end, and from what he'd heard, Spanish Mike didn't like loose ends.

5

RUNNING

The next morning, Friday, John rolled to the edge of the bed and sat up. Seven-thirty a.m. His lower back ached, his left shoulder was sore, and he had a throbbing pain behind his left eye. He glanced at the .38 still sitting on the pillow. It all flooded back. Spanish Mike's people would be looking for his body. When they got tired of looking—if they hadn't already given up—they'd start looking for him. It was time to change things up. He'd been one step behind all day yesterday. Today he intended to get way out ahead and stay there. He got dressed in his dirty clothes and drank a glass of water before he walked across the deserted parking lot to the motel office. The only evidence of the previous evening was the party trash drifting across the pavement and the empty liquor bottles lying against the curb. A new man sat behind the counter in the office, a goateed Latino who could have played linebacker before he went to fat.

"Hey," John said. "I'm down in room 98."

The receptionist turned from the computer, but he didn't stand up.

"Can I get a razor and some shaving cream?"

"Five dollars."

John took the money out of his pocket. The receptionist stood up, reached under the counter, and produced a disposable razor and a sample-size shaving cream. Then he sat back down and turned back to the computer screen.

"Thanks," John said.

John went back to his room, pulled his shirt off, and looked in the bathroom mirror. The bruises looked worse than they had last night. His rubbed his beard. It wasn't long, but it was thick. He splashed water onto it, rubbed in the shaving cream, and made the first pass over his face with the razor, rinsing the hair out of the razor after every inch or so. Then he rinsed his face and lathered up again. This time it was more like normal shaving, and even though the blade was dull, he only nicked himself twice. If Spanish Mike's men were looking for a bearded guy, they weren't going to find him.

He put his shirt back on and put the gun in his pants pocket. Then he called a cab to meet him on the street two blocks away. The morning air felt good. His headache had gone away, and his body began to loosen up as he moved. It turned out that the address he'd given to the cab company was an Asian grocery that wasn't open yet. He stood there, hunched over in his torn clothes, his hands in his pockets until the cab arrived. The cab driver, an elderly black man, lowered his window. "How I know you can pay for the ride?" he asked.

John held up a twenty-dollar bill.

"Get in," the cabbie said.

The cab dropped him at the Mail N More, which anchored a discount store strip mall near the downtown. The young man behind the counter, busy taping a box, barely noticed him. He went straight to his rented locker and collected his escape packet: driver's license, credit cards, $5,000 in cash. Just looking at the manila envelope made him feel more optimistic. This day was shaping up. He left the Mail N More and turned into the strip mall. The Goodwill was just opening up. He bought a new set of clothes: khaki pants, green golf shirt, dark blue jacket. He changed clothes in the bathroom of a MacDonald's, ate a sausage and egg biscuit, drank a cup of coffee. Now he was a completely different man.

He took another cab to an Enterprise car rental, used his new ID and credit card—he was Bryan Samson now—and left in a white Kia Rio. It was smaller than he liked to drive, but a lot less conspicuous. Time to find out just how bad his situation was. He drove across town to his apartment. A rusty, red Ford Bronco was parked in the lot across from his Cadillac. One of the men from last night sat in the driver's seat, smoking a cigarette, not even trying to hide.

John drove to another strip mall where he knew there was a Verizon store. He bought a new smart phone. He sat in the Rio in the Verizon parking lot and opened the web browser on the phone. He needed to warn Nicole, but he didn't know her phone number, and he knew that the phone number for Denison's beach house was unlisted. He surfed the web for contacts that might be helpful and found a phone number for Samantha Bartel on LinkedIn. She was exactly the kind of person who could find out Denison's phone number, and she owed him a favor.

Samantha answered her phone on the third ring. "Sam? Joe Campbell. How's life?"

"Surprised to hear from you."

"I bet."

"It's been a few years."

"That long?"

"You were lucky to catch me. We're on our way out."

"We? Has your life changed for the better?"

"Yeah, well."

"Good for you. Listen, I won't keep you. I just called because I need a favor."

"What kind of favor?"

"You still a boss over at Leapfrog Technologies?"

"I'm listening."

"I need to reach Tess. I've lost my phone, so I don't have her number, but I know where she is. That number's unlisted. Can you call there and give her my number?"

"Find an unlisted number and call Tess? That's all?"

"Yeah."

"This is for real?"

"Just give her my number. And tell her to get a new phone. If someone else answers, ask for Nicole."

"Nicole?"

"Yeah, that's what she goes by now. Could you get it done today? It's kind of important."

"I'll get it done in the next few hours."

John gave her the address of Denison's beach house. "This makes us even."

"Then I'll get it done even sooner."

John slipped his phone into his pants pocket. There was nothing else he could do here. He wanted to see Robertson on his knees; he wanted to hear him beg, but with Spanish Mike's people after him, revenge was going to have to wait. He couldn't chance the airport. They would certainly be waiting there. He had a full day of driving ahead of him. He pulled out of the lot and drove for the nearest freeway.

LATER THAT AFTERNOON, at the beach house, Nicole stood at the counter in the kitchen, cutting cauliflower into bite-size pieces and arranging them on a platter with carrots, celery, and a dish of dill dip. The phone rang. She yelled out to the den, "I got it." She rinsed her hands, dried them on the kitchen towel, and picked up the receiver. "Denisons."

"Could I speak with Nicole, please?"

"This is she."

"Nicole? Samantha Bartel."

"Sam, is that really you? It's been a long time." She looked through from the kitchen into the den, where Bell and Denison were watching a baseball game on the TV. "How have you been?"

"I'm well. I was made permanent director of new development just after you left."

"We heard you had. It's what you always wanted."

"It has its challenges, but life is good."

"Great. What's up?"

"Joe called. He wanted me to give you his new phone number."

"He lose his phone?"

"I guess. And he wants you to get a new phone."

"He didn't say why?"

"No."

"That's for the best." Nicole found a pad of paper and a pencil in a drawer. "Okay. I'm ready for the number."

Sam gave her the phone number.

"Got it. Thanks for giving me the message. Keep the new number, just in case."

Nicole set down the receiver, took out her smartphone and turned it off before she carried the snack tray through to the den. Denison and Bell were side-by-side on the love seat that faced the flat-screen TV. Nicole set the tray down on the bamboo table in front of them.

"Thanks," Bell said. She reached for a piece of celery.

Denison glanced up at Nicole. "Sit down, honey. The game is just heating up."

"Baseball's not my thing," Nicole said. "I'm going into town. Need anything?"

"Where you going?"

"I'm going to buy a new phone."

"Right now?"

"The urge just came over me. Want to come along?"

"Looking for something new or just an upgrade?"

"Upgrade."

"I'd really rather watch the game." He reached for a baby carrot and dipped it in the dill dip. "Thanks for making the snack. Take the Explorer. The keys are in it."

Nicole drove down the sandy asphalt of their neighborhood and out onto the palm-tree-lined Lighthouse Boulevard, which followed the shore. Traffic was stop-and-go. The public parking for the beaches was full. Cars were even parked on the shoulder of the road.

It seemed like there were festivals, markets, or sporting events every weekend of the summer, and this one was no exception. The Toyota RAV4 in front of her pulled over for no apparent reason. She tapped her horn and swerved around it.

How much trouble was John in? He had to be on the run. New phone and new number meant the old phone, and every phone associated with it, was compromised. She had wanted to call John's new number from the kitchen phone, just to be sure he was all right, but until she knew that the new phone was completely clean, she couldn't chance putting Denison's home phone—and Denison—at risk.

The Verizon store was on an access road next to a Burrito Boys across the boulevard from the beach in the new commercial area. There were only two cars parked in front. The greeter didn't even bother to take her name; he just waved her over to the counter. In thirty minutes, she had a new smartphone with a new number and her address book loaded. Then she drove around to the side of the building, facing out so that she could watch the entry, and called John's new number.

"John?"

"Hey, honey, how are you?" he asked.

"Better than you, I take it. Reaching out to Sam."

"She's far enough in the background to be safe."

"What happened?"

John told her everything, beginning with the appearance of Molly's boyfriend.

"Christ, honey, this is what happens when you work with amateurs. You know better."

"You can't help rubbing it in, can you? It was a simple little deal. I didn't think it would be a problem."

"Evidently. I'll be out on the next flight."

"No. I just called to give you the heads up. My name's Bryan Samson now. I'm already on the road. I'll let you know my new location when I'm sure I've lost them."

"Are you sure you're okay?"

"I'll be fine."

MEANWHILE, back at the beach house, Denison and Bell were still watching the baseball game. It was in the eighth inning, and it was all too clear that the San Francisco Giants were going to lose. Denison made a face and turned off the TV. "They can't catch a break this year."

Bell smiled. "You could root for the Marlins, instead."

"Fat chance."

She picked up the vegetable tray to carry it back into the kitchen. Denison followed her. "I've got something I want to talk to you about."

She set the tray on the granite island. "What's up?"

"Nicole asked me not to bring this up, but she told me you had a talk with her while I was out golfing."

"We both talked."

"I'm not trying to make you out to be the bad guy."

"Okay."

"I just want to clear things up. Nobody is going to replace your mom. She'll always be at the center of my heart. Thirty-five years of memories; your mother, for Christ's sakes. I can't imagine loving anyone more than her."

Bell's eyes teared up.

"Do you think I cheated on your mom?"

"You were with Nicole in Nohamay City before Mom died."

"Is that what this is about? Really, Bell? I never had sex with Nicole in Nohamay City. I was complete faithful to your mother, always, until after the funeral. Do you believe me?"

Bell nodded.

"You don't have to be jealous for your mom. Do you think she'd want that?"

Bell bit her lips and shook her head.

"And you don't have to worry about me. Your trust fund is doing fine. There will be more money when we settle your mom's estate.

And I've got more money than I could ever possibly spend. Nothing bad is going to happen."

"Your behavior is different, Dad."

"Of course it's different. So is yours. So is Skip's. Your mother was taken from us. We have to figure out how to live without her."

She sighed. "I probably shouldn't tell you this. Skip is afraid, maybe, that you had a brain bleed or something from all the pressure of taking care of Mom."

Denison shook his head. "Your brother. I never should have let him go to medical school. He hasn't stopped trying to diagnose me since his second year. Remember when he was sure you were pregnant?"

Bell laughed. "When I was bingeing on junk food freshman year? First Mom was yelling at me. Then she was yelling at him."

Denison put his hands on her shoulders and looked into her eyes. "I'm not crazy, so stop making me crazy. I enjoy being with Nicole, and I'm going to be with her. Okay?"

"Okay."

She put her arms around him. "I love you, Daddy."

"I love you too."

6

THE NEW JOB

S panish Mike, dressed in golf clothes, was riding in the front seat passenger's side of a Cadillac Escalade. "Pull over there." He pointed to a gravel lot on the side of the road where a red Ford Bronco was parked. Frankie pulled in. Spanish Mike climbed out and walked over to Knife Tattoo, who was standing under the shade of a large oak tree next to a concrete picnic table. Down the hill was the Golden Oaks Country Club. Across the fairway, they could see the clubhouse. The parking lot was full, and the noise from the children at the swimming pool carried on the breeze. "What have you got for me?"

"It's not so good, Spanish. We staked out his place, but he never came back. His car is still in the lot, loaded up just like it was when we picked him up on Thursday."

"But he's alive?"

"We combed both banks of the creek all the way down to the shallows. We never found his body. Showed his picture around town. Thursday night and Friday day receptionists at the Sunrise Motel both IDed him. So, yeah, he's alive. After that, we don't know. He probably left town."

Spanish Mike's face flushed red. "Probably? We don't know what this guy knows. You and your people are going to be knocking on doors like Jehovah's Witnesses trying to make a quota. You're going to find this guy wherever he's gone, and you're going to make him dead."

"Where do we start?"

"Reach out to our friends statewide. Motels and restaurants on the freeway. Pawn shops. Car lots. Gun sellers. He's got to get a gun, doesn't he? How much thinking have I got to do for you? Get it done."

LATER IN THE AFTERNOON, Rudy Grissom, Kevin Johnson, and Chris Billings sat in their work clothes at a small table near the bar in the Goldminer's Club. It was thirty minutes before opening. The lights were turned down, and the stage was already lit up for the first dancer. The bartender, a heavyset man in his sixties who wore a two-tone cowboy shirt and suspenders, was behind the bar checking over his stock.

"It's going to be slow tonight," Grissom said. "Too many people went to the shore."

"Good," Johnson said. "I'd like a nice quiet evening."

"Not too quiet," Billings said. "Don't want to be bored."

"Well, how about not beating anybody up tonight?"

Billings shrugged. "That's up to them. They follow the rules, I leave them alone."

Grissom's phone rang. It was Fred Stein. "Hey, Fred. I was wondering when I was going to hear from you."

"Those guys still willing to help?"

"Definitely. You find out what's she's up to?"

"No, but I've had a chance to think about what you said."

"Good for you."

"I'm going to find a place for us to set up at," Stein said. "That'll take a couple of days."

"So when do you need us?"

"Maybe a week."

"We'll be ready."

"We're just going to get the money. We're not going to hurt

anybody."

"That's why we're going to be ready. They see we're serious, they cooperate, nobody gets hurt."

"I'll be in touch."

"Looking forward to it."

Grissom ended the call. A hundred thousand dollars. It wasn't surprising that Sally could con Fred. He'd fall for anything. "We're in business, guys. Don't make any plans for next weekend."

"Still going to stiff Stein?" Johnson asked.

Grissom nodded.

"How we going to split the money?" Billings asked.

"I set it up, so I take fifty thousand. You two take twenty-five apiece."

"How about forty–thirty?" Billings asked.

"This isn't a negotiation. You're either in or out. Plenty of guys will come on board for twenty-five."

"Jesus, Rudy," Billings said. "Don't get your feelings hurt. I'm in."

THAT EVENING, Bell, Denison, and Nicole were on the sidewalk in front of the Sea Lane Chophouse. All of the outdoor seating was full, servers moving among the white-clothed, candle-lit tables, and the entry to the restaurant was crowded with walk-ins.

"Told you this place was popular," Denison said. "Let me check on our reservation." He squeezed his way through the crowd.

"Have you eaten here before?" Bell asked.

"First week I was here," Nicole said. "The pork is excellent. And they know how to mix a drink. We sat over there." She pointed to a table with a good view of the water.

"I can't remember what this place used to be."

"Your dad said it used to be Italian."

Denison reappeared. "They're ready for us."

Bell's phone rang. It was Skip. "You go ahead. I'll just be a minute."

"Should we order you a drink?" Nicole asked.

"Get me whatever you're having," Bell replied.

She stepped away from the entrance and answered her phone. "Hey, Skip. Can't talk long. I'm on the sidewalk in front of a restaurant."

"Okay. Just wanted to see how you're holding up."

"I'm fine."

"How's it going with Dad?"

"Really? It's kind of surreal. We're doing all the silly stuff we usually do at the beach, but instead of me, Dad, and Mom, it's me, Dad, the ghost of Mom, and Nicole."

"But she hasn't done anything that shows bad intent?"

"No."

"So you're telling me..."

"If Dad had met Nicole a year after Mom passed, instead of while Mom was still in the hospital, I'd be happy for them."

"Even though she's a criminal?"

"This may sound crazy, but the more I'm around her, the harder it is to remember that."

"So how long do you think they've been sleeping together?"

"Dad insists he was faithful to Mom until after the funeral, and I believe him."

"You asked him?"

"He offered it up."

"I still don't trust her."

"I know. I'm still a little angry. But there's no way we can break them up. They'll either break up themselves, or we'll have to make our peace."

"I'm not ready."

"I know it's hard. But I'm not going to blame her for stuff that's not her fault. If Dad didn't want her here, she wouldn't be here."

"Sounds like you're changing your mind."

"Look, Skip, Dad's going to do what he wants to do."

"That's what worries me."

"I've got to go. They're waiting for me at the table."

"Okay. Just keep me in the loop."

The inside of the restaurant was dimly lit and loud, with the noise of dozens of conversations. The surfaces were polished brass and dark wood. Pictures of sailing ships hung on the walls. It took Bell a few moments to spot her dad and Nicole. She weaved her way through the tables. There was a martini waiting at her place.

"Was that Bobby?" Denison asked.

"It was Skip." She took a drink.

"Is everything okay?"

"He just wanted to check in."

"You mean he was checking up."

Bell rolled her eyes. "You're not putting me in the middle, okay?"

"Okay."

"We've been having a fun day, and I just want to keep having a fun day."

Nicole lifted her martini. "I'll drink to that."

Bell picked up her menu. "Have you decided what you're going to eat?"

Six days later, John, now Bryan, sat in a booth in a mom-and-pop diner with an egg-smeared plate in front of him. Across the potholed parking lot was the Family 8, the rundown motel he'd stayed at the night before. He'd spent the last week zigzagging between towns. He'd changed cars twice. Now he was driving a tan Camry he bought from a used car lot. He sipped his second cup of coffee. He was feeling very, very safe. He got out his phone and called Nicole. "I'm in the clear."

"You sure?"

"Baby, you know that getting away is one of my best skills. Zeb reached out. He liked the money he made on that bank job so much that he tipped me to an easy score."

"Johnny, so soon? Come on."

"It's Bryan now, honey. I didn't make any money in Springville and running is expensive. Besides, this is one of Zeb's jobs. His info is always gold."

"I'm at the beach house. The cell reception isn't so good here. You better call me when you need me."

"I won't need any help on this one. It's just a little switcheroo. I'll be fine."

"That's what you said about the fiasco in Springville. I'm not kidding. Call me if you need me."

Bryan chuckled. "Are you trying to find a way to get away from there?"

"No."

"Still having trouble with the daughter?"

"Bell and I aren't best friends yet, but I'm back in James's bedroom, and she isn't fussing about it, so that's progress."

"You'll win her over. It's what you do."

"We'll see. I might have to settle for a standoff."

"I find that hard to believe. Anyway, I'll be in Martinsburg later today. That's where I'm meeting the client. I'll fill you in as soon as I know the specifics."

"You better."

"Say, you see the Save-U-Mart guy anymore?"

"No."

"You get that gun?"

"Haven't had time."

"You need to make time. You only need a gun when you haven't got one."

"Love you."

"Love you too."

Bryan put his phone in his pocket. The heat was already shimmering off the concrete. He signaled his waitress, a teenager in a dirty apron. "Can I get my check and a cup of coffee to go?"

"Yes, sir," she said.

AT MIDNIGHT, Bryan pushed through the door to The Dugout, a strip-mall sports bar. Flat-screen TVs were playing the available games and sports news programs. A few people were seated at the tables with empty pitchers, and a young couple in T-shirts and jeans sat next to each other on one side of a booth holding hands. The man whispered something to the woman. She giggled and covered her mouth with her free hand. No one was seated at the bar. Bryan took a place between two barstools and nodded toward the bartender, a pudgy guy with silver-gray hair and a cauliflower ear.

"We're done serving," the bartender said.

"I'm looking for Stanley."

"That's me."

"You own this bar?"

"Yep. What's this about?"

"We've got a mutual friend who told me I should come see you about a project you're planning. Can you name that friend?"

Stanley nodded slowly. "Zeb."

Bryan stuck out his hand. "Pleased to meet you, Stanley."

"And what do I call you?"

"Ernie." Bryan leaned forward and whispered. "I understand you want to rob a gambling operation—that you're the inside man."

Stanley held up a hand. "Let me get closed." He stepped out from behind the bar and started walking to the door. "Time to go, folks. Thanks for stopping by."

Bryan didn't turn around. He put his elbows on the bar and waited. He heard chairs scraping the floor, voices making comments that he couldn't understand, and the door opening and shutting. Then Stanley came back behind the bar.

"Something to drink?"

"No, thanks."

"Okay, then. There's a backroom game here every Monday. We're closed. Same people every week. They come in, trade their cash for chips, the cash goes in the safe. When the game is over, everybody cashes out."

"How much?"

"About forty thousand, give or take."

"That's a big game for a Monday night."

"Four tables of six if everyone shows."

"Twenty-four players? So you want to stage a robbery during the game?"

"That's about the size of it."

"Any of the players carry guns?"

"They're not supposed to."

"A lot of risk in a robbery. To believe it, the people have to see it. They don't see it, and you're not dead, they think you're in on it. But if they see it, somebody might do something foolish and get themselves —or us—shot."

"Look, Ernie, Zeb told me you were the man for the job. I figured you'd come in here with some masked guys and make it convincing, but if you don't want to do it..."

"Relax, Stanley. I didn't say I wouldn't help you. I'm just thinking about the best way. How about we replace the money with counterfeit instead of faking a robbery."

"Counterfeit?"

"Yeah."

"That hadn't crossed my mind. It would have to look just like real money."

"You won't be able to tell the difference. Nobody pointing fingers, blaming your security. They're all back next week. Best of all, nobody's accidentally killed."

"So how would that work?"

"We buy the counterfeit—It'll cost five thousand..."

"Five thousand?"

"Nothing's free—which leaves at least thirty-five thousand that we divide in half. You good with that?"

"I'm taking the risk. I'm the one who could get caught. I should get more."

"And I'm the one who's managing your risk almost all the way down to zero. That's why you pay me."

Stanley thought for a minute. "Okay. This counterfeit is going to look like real money?"

"Exactly."

"Then we're on."

7

COUNTERFEIT

The next morning Fred Stein stood on Rainy Street in front of a house in the spring break rental zone of Cricket Bay. All of the houses in this neighborhood had missing screens, peeling paint, and sagging porches. The yards were patchy grass and weeds. Crushed beer cans and smashed take-out containers seemed to have crawled under every bush. Since the summer season was almost over, most of the houses in this neighborhood were already empty. This house's particular virtue was that a previous owner had jacked it up eight feet after a bad storm surge and then enclosed the open space to make what was essentially an above-ground basement.

Stein put the keys into his front pocket. This place would do nicely. It was a furnished three-bedroom. They could use it as their base of operations before they got the money from Sally, and if they needed to hold one of her people, they could put them down in the faux basement. A toilet, a sink, and no windows. He got into his Corolla and took out his cellphone. "Carrie? It's Fred."

"When are you coming home?"

"I've got a new lead."

"Honey, I know you say you're trying as hard as you can, but it's getting harder and harder to believe you."

"Carrie, honey…"

"Don't 'Carrie, honey' me. You need to tell me the truth. Getting my hopes up is not an action plan."

He took a deep breath. "Okay. This is the way it is: every job I apply for, I get rejected as soon as they find out about my conviction."

"I can't keep shouldering this load alone. I'm exhausted. You need to come home and take any job you can get. Even a fast-food job would help."

"I was going to surprise you, but I actually do have a lead on some money."

"From where?"

"You remember how everyone scattered after I was arrested? I tracked down one of those guys."

"I don't want you to do anything illegal."

"This isn't illegal."

"It's just not worth it."

"This is money I earned fair and square."

"How much?"

"Sixty thousand."

"Sixty thousand dollars? That you earned fair and square?"

"My hand to God."

"You earned sixty thousand dollars fair and square, but you had to track down this guy to get paid. You can see how fishy that sounds."

"It's the truth."

"When will you get it?"

"I'll have this money within the week."

She sighed. "Okay. Not a day longer. With or without this money you're coming home. I need you here."

"I'll be there."

"And no more lies. You're in the doghouse until I can be sure of you."

She ended the call. Stein sat behind the steering wheel looking at the face of his phone. The home invasion was the right choice. Finally, he was going to catch a break.

NICOLE SAT out on the swimming pool deck talking on the phone with Bryan. The day was overcast, and the surf was choppy. The breeze felt cool for August. She pulled her beach cover-up around her shoulders and tried to button it one-handed.

"So that's about the size of it," he said.

"Sounds simple enough."

"There are no moving parts to this one. Monday evening I'll make the swap and leave town."

"You don't have the counterfeit yet."

"True, but this is Zeb's connection, so it should all go smooth. Don't worry. Since my midnight swim my paranoia has paranoia."

"That's the way it should always be." Nicole saw some sunshine peeking through the clouds in the distance.

"So how are things with you?"

"Like I told you yesterday, Bell's still softening, but she's only here another ten days. We don't have much in common, and I'm not sleeping with *her*, so all in all I think I'm doing pretty well. Playing everything honest just makes this a tougher sell."

"Honesty is the hardest game. There's not much room to spin."

"Exactly, manipulating a web of lies is child's play, but a web of truth? It requires too much trust."

"Yeah, but it's the only approach that's going to work over the long run."

"So what are you going to do after you finish this job?"

"Jump around for a week, and then find a place to relax."

"I love you. You be careful."

"I love you too."

Nicole walked back into the kitchen. She could see Denison in the mudroom in his golf clothes, his golf shoes in one hand. "There you are," she said. "Where's Bell?"

"In the garage."

"How was golf?"

"I'm getting old." He set his golf shoes on a shelf by the door to the garage.

"She give you a run for your money?"

"She'll be in here bragging in a minute. What have you been doing?"

"Talking to John."

He studied her face. "Are you leaving?"

"No, we've just been catching up. He should have asked for my help, but didn't. Ran into a bit of trouble. His name's Bryan now."

"Bryan?"

"Yeah."

He put his hands on her hips and kissed her. "As long as he doesn't need you, I don't care what his name is."

BRYAN DROVE his Camry into the U-Store Self Storage located half a block from the south loop interstate interchange in Martinsburg. Even though it was just midmorning, he had the windows up and the air-conditioning on. He drove down the rows of storage units until he came to unit 212. A black man wearing blue work clothes with the name *Marty* embroidered on the shirt pocket was waiting for him. Bryan got out of the Camry carrying a red book bag in one hand. "Good morning."

The black man eyed him suspiciously. "Am I supposed to know you?"

"Zeb told me that you'd have something for me."

"What's your name?"

"I'm the Traveling Man."

Marty grunted, then turned and unlocked the garage door to the storage unit and rolled it up. On the concrete floor in the unit was a single cardboard box. "It's five thousand for the fifty grand."

"Five? Zeb said three."

"Did he?" Marty grimaced. "I'll split the difference. Four thousand."

Bryan set the book bag on the floor and squatted to open the flaps on the cardboard box. Fifty thousand in counterfeit bills. He reached in, pulled out a banded bundle, pulled a bill out at random and held it up to the light. "Very nice work."

"My guy knows his way around a press."

Bryan counted $1,000 out of his pocket, added it to the book bag with the three thousand, and tossed the bag to Marty. "That makes four thousand."

Marty poked through the money in the bag. "We're good."

"How do I get in touch when I need more?"

Marty shook his head. "No disrespect, but I don't know you. I know a guy you know, which is not the same thing. So you get in touch with Zeb if you need me."

"Fair enough." Bryan picked up the cardboard box.

Marty left the book bag in the storage unit and pulled down the garage door. He watched Bryan get back into his car and drive away. Then he got out his phone.

"Hey, Frankie. That dude you're looking for? The con man? He was just here."

"Really?"

"No doubt. He's driving a tan Camry. I'm texting you a picture of the license plate."

"We owe you one."

"No problem. Always looking to help a friend."

THAT NIGHT A STORM rolled in from the ocean. At first the rain pitter-pattered on the windows, but then the wind picked up, and the rain pounded the glass. Bell lay in bed on her side, a pillow between her legs and her phone against her ear, talking to Bobby. "Hang on, I can't hear you." She adjusted the volume on her phone. "That should do it. Anyway, I'm sorry I have to keep talking this through."

"That's okay. It's a lot to take in," Bobby replied. "Are you getting any closure?"

"Yeah, I guess so. I've got Skip off my back."

"That's a start."

"And Nicole isn't evil, and Dad was faithful."

"But?"

"This is a strange thing to say, but even though Nicole is kind and takes good care of Dad, and she's not jealous of my relationship with him, I don't think she's good enough for him."

"So she's in the same category as Skip's wife."

"I didn't say that."

He chuckled. "But you don't think any women are good enough for your men."

She smiled. "Because they aren't."

"It's a good thing your brother and your dad aren't as picky as you. They would have gotten rid of me by now."

She shifted onto her back. "I miss you so much."

"I miss you more."

She touched herself. "Do you want to play telephone?"

"I thought you didn't want to do that anymore."

"I changed my mind."

"I'm game. I'm walking toward the bedroom. Do you want me to be me or someone else?"

"You."

"Are you a good girl or a bad girl?"

"I'm a bad, bad girl."

"What are you wearing?"

"I'm wearing the dress I was wearing when we went to Jeremy and Stella's party. Do you remember it?"

"Oh, yeah. The supermodel dress. You looked...incredible. I could barely keep my hands off you."

"Do you remember what we did in the car at the top of the hill?"

"Do I ever."

"Start there."

8

THE KIDNAPPING

On Sunday afternoon, Fred Stein stood on the porch of the rental house on Rainy Street as his old friend Rudy Grissom came up the sidewalk with the two men he'd recruited to help recover the money. "Rudy, glad to see you."

Grissom pointed to the large black man wearing pirate earrings. "This is Kevin Johnson."

Johnson flashed a smile.

Then Grissom pointed to the muscled-up blond guy with flat, dull eyes. Stein thought he looked like trouble. "This is Chris Billings."

Stein shook hands with them both.

Grissom slapped Stein on the shoulder. "They work at the club. They're reliable guys."

"Glad you guys could come," Stein said. "Let's go inside."

Stein unlocked the door and led the way. The house was open from front to back, with a hallway to the bedrooms and bathroom to the left. The living room held a well-worn sofa, two chairs, a coffee table, and a flat-screen TV. Next came a dining room table with four chairs. The kitchen was separated from the rest of the room by a bar height Formica countertop.

"Nice-looking place," Grissom said.

Stein gestured toward the dining area. "How about we sit at the table?"

They all sat down. "Everything set?" Grissom asked.

Stein looked from Billings to Johnson. "You done this sort of thing before?"

"Rudy has filled us in," Johnson said, "but we'd like to hear it from you."

"Long story short," Stein said, "I bumped into this woman who ripped me off a few years ago. She's a grifter. I've been following her. She's staying with a man and a woman. I checked the property records and did an Internet search. The guy, James Denison, is a millionaire. Loaded big time. He's either in with them on some scam or they're manipulating him. Either way is good for us. We threaten them, take him to the bank, he gets us the money."

Billings frowned. "So you're talking home invasion. I've done some of those. They can get messy."

"They'll cooperate. She's a player. They can't go to the police."

"What makes you think they won't just come after us?" Johnson asked.

"I know her. That's not her style. She doesn't want to attract any attention to herself. As long as she knows no one's going to get hurt if she pays, she's going to pay."

"And we get five grand?" Johnson asked.

"Five apiece," Stein said.

"Out of one hundred grand?" Billings asked.

"Yeah," Grissom said. "But you're being hired to do a job. You get paid no matter what."

"What if they don't have the cash on hand?" Johnson asked.

"That's why I rented this place," Stein said. "We'll take one of them hostage and put them in the downstairs here."

"So when are we going to do this?" Billings asked.

"Tomorrow is Monday," Stein continued. "We hit them just before the banks open. And another thing. I don't want any violence. Anyone gets hurt, everything gets complicated. We don't want that. Can you guys go with that?"

"Absolutely," Johnson nodded.

"For five grand, I'm not going to let anyone hurt me," Billings said. "But if they're cool, I can be cool."

"Okay then," Stein said.

Grissom scooted his chair back. "What did I tell you? This is going to work out just fine."

THE NEXT MORNING, shortly after 9:00 a.m., Denison, Bell, and Nicole sat around the kitchen island drinking coffee and eating breakfast. They were already dressed for the day—Denison in golf clothes, Bell in a yellow-and-green striped sundress, and Nicole in shorts and a sleeveless top. The doorbell rang. Denison walked through to the entryway to answer the door. Four men in dark clothes with automatic pistols down at their sides stood on the front steps: a blocky, gray-haired man with an acne-scarred face, a large black man with gold hoop earrings, a blond man with spiky hair, and a sloppy fat man with a thin comb-over.

Denison's mouth gaped open. He tried to slam the door shut, but they shoved their way in. He recognized the fat man. "Hey! You're the guy from Jerry's Surf House. Fred—Fred what's his name."

"I've come for my money."

"I don't want any trouble," Denison said.

"That's great," Acne Scars said, "because we don't want to have to clean up after any trouble. You do what we say, everything will turn out fine. Where are the women?"

"In the kitchen."

They pushed him back through the house. "Look at this place," the black guy said. "They definitely have the cash."

Nicole appeared in the hallway. "Oh, no."

She'd witnessed this scene too many times before. She spun on her heels, but the blond guy grabbed her arm and pushed his pistol into her side. "Easy now, honey pie."

Bell jumped off her stool as they came into the kitchen. Stein pointed his gun. She yelped.

"Sit back down. Everybody take a seat," Stein said.

Denison, Bell, and Nicole sat on the stools at the island. The intruders stood around them, guns in their hands, all hard looks and intimidation. "How this goes is up to you, Sally," Stein said. "You play it easy, and no one will get hurt, I promise you. I admit that two years ago I wanted to kill you, but now it's just about the money. You give us one hundred thousand, and we go right back out that door."

Nicole looked the intruders over, sizing them up. She knew that Stein was soft—that he was easy to fool and couldn't run a crew. If he was in charge, she couldn't think of a single reason why she should admit anything. "Mister, I told you before, I'm not Sally. I'm Nicole Carter. I don't know what I could do to convince you, but you have to believe me."

"Sally Jones. That's your name. Or that's what you told me your name was. Maybe it was Nicole Carter all along."

"I've never met you before."

"Fred," Acne Scars said, "this is going nowhere. Let's separate them and see how long they can keep their stories straight. We can take her." He pointed to Nicole. "Mr. Black can take him." He nodded toward the black guy and pointed to Denison. "And Mr. White can take her." He nodded toward the blond guy and pointed to Bell.

Mr. White grinned. "It'll be my pleasure." He took hold of Bell's arm. She tried to pull away.

Nicole glanced from Stein to Acne Scars to Mr. Black and finally to Mr. White. It looked like Acne Scars was the brains. Mr. Black moved quickly enough, but she bet he was just here to get paid. Mr. White, on the other hand, had the pitiless look of a predator. He'd probably enjoy smacking Bell around. Nicole couldn't allow that to happen. She was going to have to change tack. "Okay," Nicole held up one hand. "Okay, I do know who you are."

Acne Scars leaned back against the refrigerator. "That's better."

"But these two don't have the slightest idea what you're talking about. I just met them a couple of months ago."

Stein snorted. "They aren't your partners?"

"No."

"So you're working them?"

Nicole drew out her answer as if she didn't want to say it. "Yeah, okay, I've been working them. You put a wrinkle in my plan when you bumped into us a couple of weeks ago."

"What?" Bell glared at her. "I was beginning to trust you."

"Settle down, honey," Denison said.

Stein continued. "How much were you taking them for?"

Nicole swallowed hard. "Everything."

"Meaning what?" Acne Scars asked.

She looked down at the granite counter. She hoped Denison knew what she was doing. "If everything went according to plan, he'd be proposing to me in the next week or two. Six months from now, I'd be Mrs. Denison."

Denison acted confused and angry. "Really? You don't love me? I can't believe this."

"Skip was right all along," Bell said.

Stein smiled. "That's the Sally I know." He turned to Denison. "You're lucky I came along. I saved you a lot of grief. That's worth a hundred thousand easy."

"So there's no reason to involve them," Nicole said. "Let's get out of here, and we'll see what we can work out."

Acne Scars, Mr. Black, and Mr. White exchanged glances. "No way," Acne Scars said.

"They're not my partners," Nicole said.

"Who cares?" Mr. Black replied.

"What do you mean?" Stein asked.

"Don't worry about it," Acne Scars continued. "In the end, we don't care if they're connected. Does she have one hundred thousand? He's the one with the money. He's in a bad place, and he's going to pay."

"I get you," Stein said. He turned to Denison. "You want your life back? Call the bank and arrange for our money."

"What if I won't do it?"

"You have to go to the bank, so we can't mark you up," Acne Scars said. He gestured at Nicole. "And you don't care about her. She's just a grifter. So that leaves the princess. We don't want to hurt her, but that's up to you."

The color drained from Bell's face. She stammered. Denison shushed her. "I'll do it."

"And no funny business," Acne Scars said. "Put it on speaker."

Denison called the bank.

"Good morning. ECB Bank. How can I direct your call?"

"Hello, this is James Denison. Is Cory Davids available?"

"One moment, please."

There was a short pause.

"Cory Davids."

"Cory? How are you? This is James Denison. The reason I've called is that I need one hundred thousand dollars, cash."

"Cash? Wow. Could you take a cashier's check?"

"No, it's got to be cash."

"Mr. Denison, there's extra government reporting for a cash withdrawal of that size. Are you in trouble? Should I call the police?"

"I'm not in trouble, and I don't need the police. I need one hundred thousand dollars in cash."

"Okay, Mr. Denison. I'll assemble the cash for you, but it's going to take a few days."

"A few days?"

"Everything's electronic nowadays. We don't keep that much extra money around, so I'll have to have it brought in. That takes time."

"I need the money as soon as possible. Can't you speed things up?"

"Hang on a minute." There was a short pause. "Mr. Denison?"

"Yeah."

"I can't promise, but I'm going to do everything I can to assemble the money before ten a.m. tomorrow."

"Tomorrow? Can't you get the money together sooner than that?"

"I'm afraid not. That's the absolute best we can do."

"Okay, then. Call me as soon as you have the money." Denison hung up the phone.

"That's bullshit," Acne Scars said.

"You heard him. Trust me, I like this even less than you."

Mr. White pointed at Bell. "So we're taking her?"

"Take?" Denison asked.

"Yeah," Acne Scars said. "We're not staying here until tomorrow, so she's coming with us."

"Take me," Nicole said.

"You've got to be kidding," Acne Scars said. "If you're not partners, they got no reason to get the money."

"I'll go," Denison said.

"You need to be here in case the bank calls with questions."

Mr. Black and Mr. White pulled Bell off her stool. She started to struggle. "Do you want to get slapped?" Mr. White asked.

"You don't have to take her," Denison said. "I'll pay."

"I know you will," Acne Scars said. "One hundred thousand. You go to the bank in the morning and get the money. You do what you're told, you'll get this one back before lunch."

Bell looked at Nicole. "You did this. This is all your fault."

"You better not hurt her," Denison said.

"You don't screw around, and she'll be fine. Keep your mouth shut and get the money," Acne Scars said.

Bell started crying.

Mr. White and Mr. Black pushed Bell down the hall, Acne Scars and Stein close behind them. Denison crumpled to his knees. "Oh, my God. Oh, my God."

Nicole knelt beside him. "I'm so sorry, James."

The front door slammed. Nicole ran down the hall and looked out the window just as a blue minivan drove away. She went back to the kitchen. Denison was standing at the island with his smart phone in his hand.

"They won't hurt her, will they?"

"Not until they have the money."

Denison seemed to be having trouble taking in the information. "Not until...Not until...I'm calling the police."

"Don't do it. That's the surest way to get her killed. Think about it.

The cops find them or put a tracker on the money. Who's the first person to die in the gunfight? The hostage."

"What do we do?"

"Why don't you call your security guys; see if they can help?"

"Yeah, okay." He called Manifold Security Company and explained the situation. "They said they couldn't do anything illegal—that we should call the police, and they would walk us through it. So that's that. You sure I can't call the police?"

"I wouldn't."

"What should I do?"

"You know they aren't going to let her go, don't you? We've seen them. As soon as they have the money, we're just loose ends. They'll try to kill us all."

The color drained from his face. "Jesus."

"Look, I know Fred. He's not a psycho. He's just an opportunist. He won't hurt Bell. He'll want to treat her right to show good faith."

"But will the others do what he says?"

"You saw what happened. It looks like the guy with the acne scars is calling the shots, but he wants Fred to think he's in charge. The other guys will probably follow his lead."

"Probably?"

"That's all we've got. Bell is safe until they have the money. We've got until then to take her back."

"How?"

"Let me call Bryan."

THE BLUE MINIVAN was on Lighthouse Boulevard when the heavy clouds that had blown in earlier cut loose, and the hard rain started banging off the top of the minivan and filling the gutters on the sides of the street. Grissom and Stein were in front, Grissom driving. Johnson and Billings were in the second row. Bell sat in the back row of the minivan by herself, whimpering, her wrists cuffed behind her back.

Grissom turned on the headlights and the windshield wipers. "Can't see a thing," he said.

"The turn is just up ahead," Stein said.

Johnson glanced back at Bell. "Will you stop crying, already? We're not going to hurt you."

"Let her cry," Billings said.

"She's getting on my nerves."

"Why? Remind you of your wife?"

"You're the funny guy."

"Yeah, I am."

"Knock it off," Grissom said. "I'm trying to concentrate."

Bell lay down on her side and scrunched her eyes shut. This couldn't be happening. This was crazy, like something out of a tabloid. This kind of thing never happened to people like her. Being kidnapped. Held for ransom. It was all Nicole's fault. If she hadn't come into their lives, none of this would have happened. Bell shifted her weight. She'd been right from the very beginning. She'd tried to warn her dad. But she couldn't blame him. Nicole had fooled her too, even though she'd had her guard up, and Skip reinforcing every doubt. Nicole really was a sociopath, devious in every word and deed. Bell felt a vibration in the pocket of her sundress. Her phone. She'd forgotten all about it. How could she keep them from finding it?

She pulled at the fabric of her dress, inching along with her hand-cuffed hands, until she reached the top of the pocket. She dug down in her pocket and gripped the phone with one hand. If she could just get the phone into her underwear, maybe they wouldn't find it. She brought her knees up to her chest so that she could pull the hem of her dress up above her panties. As long as neither of the guys in the second seat looked back, she had a chance. She got a finger from one hand under the elastic of her panties and pulled them away from her skin. Then she pushed the phone in with the other hand. She could feel the phone rubbing against her bottom, but the plastic cuffs cut into her wrists, and she couldn't push the phone any farther and still hold onto her panties at the same time. She gave the phone one more push and let go of her panties. The phone popped out. Damn it. She felt around on the seat behind her. Where was it? She shifted onto her back. The two guys in front of her were still facing forward. She craned her neck to look over her shoulder, but she couldn't see the phone. The minivan braked hard. She banged against the seat back. Then she heard a quiet thump, like a small object falling onto the carpet. She rolled back onto her side and felt over every inch she could reach, but she couldn't find the phone. Tears trickled down her cheek.

NICOLE STOOD IN THE DEN, holding Denison's hand and looking out the window at the sea. She had her phone up against her ear. She was trying to call Bryan, but he hadn't picked up. Lightning struck the water in the distance, illuminating a flash of choppy waves through the storm. She waited for the thunder. One, two, three, boom. Less than a mile. The strike was closer than she thought. She glanced at the screen on her phone. She still had a connection. She put the phone back up to her ear. "Bryan?"

"I'm in the middle of something."

"Can't wait."

"What do you need?"

"Remember that guy I told you about? The fat fuck who recognized me?"

"You didn't buy the gun, did you?"

"They took Bell. They want one hundred K."

"How many are they?"

"Four."

"Good thing you didn't buy that gun, it would have just got you shot. Time for you to leave."

Nicole moved away from Denison. "What?"

"Time to let them go."

She dropped her voice. "I can't do that."

"You willing to die for her? It's all swirling in the toilet. Get out of there."

She stood in the dark kitchen looking back into the den at Denison. "*You* told me to come here," she whispered. "*You* told me to play it straight. Goddamn it, Bryan, they're in trouble because of me, and I need your help."

"Nicki, you know as well as I do that nobody can count the number of ways a rescue can go wrong, and there's only a few ways it can go right. This is a losing proposition. It's time to cut your losses. You've had a good run. It almost worked out."

"I won't leave them. If you won't help me, I'll do it alone."

"You sound serious."

"I am serious. They're real people to me."

The line was quiet except for Bryan's breathing. Nicole waited for him to speak. "Bryan?"

"Okay, baby. Okay. This is probably the stupidest thing I've ever done, but you've convinced me. Forget I ever objected. I'll line up some muscle. Tell Denison it's going to cost a few dollars. I'll call back with the details."

"Thank you."

"Keep a close watch on Denison. If he turns on you, you've got to run."

"He won't turn."

"Just the same."

She went back into the den. "Bryan's on his way. He's going to line up some help."

"What's he going to do?"

"Specifically? I don't know. But he'll know what to do. He always does."

She took Denison in her arms and whispered in his ear. "I know this is hard. Harder than even carrying the emotional load of Stacey's death because you haven't finished carrying that, and you have to carry this new weight on top of it. But you have to stay strong for Bell. You can't fall apart. She needs you right now. She's depending on you. We'll go to the bank in the morning. Make the arrangements. Bryan will get here and figure out what to do."

She let go of him. He gripped her shoulders and stared down into her eyes. "I don't know if we're doing the right thing. My God, my little girl, all alone with those bastards. Afraid for her life. She's not like you."

"She knows you're going to do everything possible. She knows you won't give up on her. That's what's going to keep her going."

He dropped his arms and looked away. "I know it's not your fault. I know you had nothing to do with this. But this wouldn't have happened if you hadn't been here."

"I know. I'm so sorry."

"I think I need to be alone for a while."

She watched him walk away. What a fucking mess. She was sure about Stein. He wouldn't be able to sleep at night if he hurt Bell. But the other guys? Particularly Acne Scars. What were his limits? Was he willing to go to any extreme, or would he back down if he feared for his life? And would Mr. Black and Mr. White follow his lead in a crisis? She looked back out the window into the storm. She hadn't been completely honest with James. She knew exactly what they were going to do after Bryan and the hired guns arrived. They were going to gear up, find Bell, and take her back. And they were going to kill anyone who got in the way.

At the rental house on Rainy Street, Stein led Bell down the stairs into the faux basement, where he cut her hands free. She shuffled into the space, her head down, as if she were in a trance.

"Cooperate, and everything will be fine. If you yell or bang to attract attention, we'll have to tie you up and gag you. We don't want to do that. We want you to be comfortable, but that's up to you. You'll be going home tomorrow. So cheer up. I'll bring you some food in a little while."

Bell looked around the room. The floor was a concrete slab, and the walls were white painted plywood. An overhead light hung from a cord plugged into a ceiling outlet. There were no windows, and the utility door was chained and padlocked. A card table, two folding chairs, a camp cot, and a sleeping bag had been set up in the middle of the space. A toilet and a sink were located next to the plumbing lines that came down from the kitchen. As soon as she heard the door lock at the top of the stairs, she shuffled to the utility door and tugged on the padlock. Locked tight. This was really happening. She glanced at her watch: 10:30. Twenty-three hours to go. She looked up the stairs to the basement door. Her legs felt rubbery, but she was afraid to sit, afraid to let down her guard for even one second. If only she had her phone. If only...*Stop that.* No more feeling sorry for herself. She had to keep her wits about her, save her energy. She didn't know what might happen, and she had to be ready.

GRISSOM and the others were already sitting around in the living room when Stein came up out of the basement. "All set?"

Stein nodded. Grissom took a beer out of an open six-pack and handed the six-pack to Johnson, who did the same before he passed it along.

"So far so good," Johnson said.

"I don't know," Stein said. "It all seems a little weird. Sally is a player without a doubt. But the princess and Denison? Maybe he is her dad."

"Doesn't matter. We're not backing out now," Grissom said. "We've gone too far."

"I didn't say we should back out. I spent two years in jail. I'm going to get my money back. What if the princess isn't in the game? That's all I'm saying."

"Then she shouldn't be hanging out with players," Grissom said. "Look, if what you say about them is true—as long as she's undamaged goods—we're going to be fine."

Billings set the half-empty six-pack on the coffee table. "Tomorrow we're going to get paid and then we're out of here. No harm, no foul."

Stein nodded. "You're right. No harm, no foul. This is really happening. Tomorrow this will be all over with."

"Easy money," Johnson said.

Bryan sat in his car in front of the Buy-N-Loan pawnshop, filling the magazine of the used Glock he'd just bought. Bell kidnapped by the guy who recognized Nicole. What a mess. Nicole should just walk away. No matter what happened, Denison was bound to blame her, at least a little bit. He might not hate her, but he certainly wouldn't want her in his bed. And if Bell were raped or murdered, Denison would definitely associate all that misery and pain with Nicole. There was no upside here. Still, he knew why she couldn't leave Denison. He'd told her to work her magic and she'd worked it on herself. Intimacy was a powerful drug, more addictive than heroin. He got out his phone. "Zeb?"

"Yeah."

"Can you get me a couple of gunslingers?"

"Gunslingers?"

"This is on a different job."

"Sorry, my go-to guys are out of pocket. How long can you wait?"

"I need them now."

"Good luck."

Bryan took a list of phone numbers out of his wallet and called the top number. No answer. He called the next one down. "Billy? It's the Traveling Man."

"What's up?"

"I need a couple of gunslingers."

"How soon?"

"Right now."

"Awful short notice, but I might have somebody. Let me call you right back."

Bryan watched the traffic in front of the pawnshop and waited. His phone rang. It was Billy. "What you got for me?"

"I've got you one guy, but he's a crazy SOB."

"Crazy in a good way or crazy in a bad way?"

"He'll keep his word, but once he's off the leash, you can't call him back."

"What's his pay scale?"

"Ten grand per gunfight."

"Per gunfight?"

"I told you he was crazy. Some kind of ex-military psycho. Don't hire him if you can't pay him."

"How soon can he get to Cricket Bay, Florida?"

"He could probably get there by tomorrow."

"No sooner?"

"He's got to travel a ways."

"Put him on a plane. Include the tickets in your fee. And one more thing. Where can I get a brand-new tool kit?"

"You've never asked me for gear before."

"I'm asking now."

"How big a kit you need?"

"Full package for three."

"It's going to cost you."

"No problem."

"I got a buddy close at hand. He'll give you a call."

"Trustworthy?"

"Family."

"Let me give you my wife's number. She's on the ground."

Bryan ended the call and then speed-dialed Nicole. "Zeb couldn't help, so I got ahold of Billy. Gunfighter and a full package are on the way. Billy'll get in touch with you about the details."

"Great. What about you? When do you get here?"

"I'll be flying out this evening. I should be there before the gunfighter."

"Why can't you come sooner?"

"I've got to finish up this little job I'm on."

"I need you now."

"Nicole, me being there won't make any difference until the gunfighter and the gear arrive. So take a deep breath. How's Denison holding up?"

"He's a mess."

"Maybe you'll get lucky, and they'll take the money and go."

"Fat chance. And Bryan, I'm sorry I barked at you. Thanks for helping. I know it's not the smart move."

"I've always got your back. We've dealt with tougher situations. See you soon."

"Love you."

"Love you."

Bryan tossed his phone into the passenger's seat. If the gunfighter was half as good as his reputation, they might have a chance. He put his car in gear. He needed to put the Cricket Bay fiasco out of his mind and focus on tonight's card game. That was today's business. He had the counterfeit money and an extra gun. If Stanley didn't double-cross him, this would be some of the easiest money he ever made. Pull the switcheroo and drive straight to the airport. Should he make a reservation? No, better to play it fast and loose. Next, he needed to pack up his motel room and take a nap. Then he'd be ready for the evening.

NICOLE FOUND Denison sitting on the unmade bed in Bell's room, looking at a laptop computer screen. His hands trembled. His eyes were hollow, and his face was gray. She sat down beside him, but he didn't say anything. "Bryan called back. Everything is in motion."

"I should call Skip and Bobby."

Nicole shook her head. "Don't do it."

"They need to know."

"Why? So they can be afraid? So they can argue with you? Would one of them go to the police behind your back? Right now, you need to save your strength. The fewer people who know the better."

"Are you sure you're right?"

"I know I'm right." She looked at the laptop. "What are you doing?"

"This is Bell's laptop." The screen showed a map of the area. A green dot was traveling down a street. "She has the 'Find My Phone' app."

"And that's her phone?"

"Yeah."

"Jimmy, this is a game-changer."

"Because we know where she is?"

"Maybe. She hasn't called, has she?"

Denison shook his head.

"So her phone is in a car."

"Where are they taking her?"

"She probably doesn't have the phone. Either one of the kidnappers has it or it's lost in the car seat."

"So what are we going to do?"

"We're going to chase it down. Maybe it will lead us to Bell. But we have to be very careful. If they spot us, it might make things worse for her. Really we should wait for Bryan, but we can't take the chance on the battery going dead."

Nicole reached across Denison to open *Finder* and look in *Applications*. "No cell service on this laptop, so we'll need to link it to the 'hotspot' on my phone."

Nicole's phone rang. "Yeah?"

"This is Billy. Gunfighter's name is Cohen. He'll arrive on the Delta flight at one o'clock tomorrow. One of my guys will call about your packages before four p.m. That's the best I could do."

"Thanks."

"Give my regards to your old man." The line went dead.

"Who was that?" Denison asked.

"The guns and the hired help get here tomorrow afternoon."

Denison sighed. "We really going to do this? Is this really the best way?"

"If the money is ready in the morning, we won't be able to stall. We'll have to trade for Bell and hope for the best. But if the timeline gets backed up, or something goes sideways, it's better to have the help and the guns and not need them than the other way around," Nicole said.

An hour later, Nicole and Denison were tracking the blue minivan as it drove through a rental neighborhood a few blocks from the public beach. When the minivan pulled into a driveway, they parked on the street about half a block down. They watched the blond guy and the black guy get out of the minivan and carry groceries up the stairs and into the house. "Our luck is holding up," Nicole said. "What did the other guy call them?"

"Mr. White and Mr. Black."

They sat watching for a while longer, but no one came out. "So this is their safe house," Nicole said. "Either Bell's in there, or one of those guys can tell us where she is."

"So now the police could help us."

She put her hand on his arm. "Yeah, if they believed us, they could roll up in there and get Bell shot. I've told you, if we want her back, we have to take her ourselves."

"Are you sure? Are you really sure? I'm putting Bell's life in your hands."

"Trust me. It's the only way. The cops will just screw it up."

"So what do we do now?"

"Wait. We know everything we can know. Maybe we get lucky in the morning. If not, we've made our preparations. Cheer up, James. We know where Bell is. That's the kind of information that's going to make all the difference if we need to move fast."

9

THE WILD CARDS

In the early evening, Bryan leaned on the bar in The Dugout sports bar, talking with Stanley. The front room was completely empty, and the overhead lights were turned off. "Cops ever come by to check why there are so many cars parked out front when you're closed?"

"I pay a gratuity to the police union."

"All the better. Everybody here?"

"Yeah."

"What's the money count?"

"Forty-two five. Mainly hundreds, but some small bills mixed in."

"I'll be back."

Bryan stood on the sidewalk in front of the bar, glancing around nonchalantly, satisfying himself that no one was watching him. He crossed the parking lot to his Camry, sat down in the back seat with a book bag containing the counterfeit money, and counted $7,500 into a grocery sack, which left $42,500 in the book bag. When he got back to The Dugout, a heavy-set bald man in gray slacks and a black sports coat was standing at the bar. The man looked over his shoulder at Bryan.

"No problem," Stanley said to the man. "Just a friend of mine." He set a mixed drink in front of the man.

"Thanks, Stan." The man took his drink into the backroom.

Bryan watched him go. "I thought everyone was already here."

"Needed a drink. Let's get this done so I can get back there to keep an eye on things."

"The counterfeit cost five grand, so I get that back, which leaves thirty-seven five profit. Divided by two, equals eighteen thousand, seven-hundred and fifty. Fair enough?"

Stanley nodded.

Bryan set the book bag on the bar. "Don't get the money mixed up, 'cause you won't be able to tell it apart."

Bryan watched as Stanley unlocked the floor safe behind the bar, counted out $23,750 into a plastic grocery bag, counted out $18,750 into another bag, and put the counterfeit money into the safe. Then he slipped the $23,750 into the book bag and set it back up on the bar.

Bryan shifted the bag onto his shoulder. "It's been great doing business with you."

The sun was low behind the nearby apartments when Bryan came out of The Dugout and climbed into his Camry. If only every job went so smoothly. Since he'd only paid $4,000 for the counterfeit, he'd made $19,750 on the deal, plus the $7,500 in extra counterfeit. Hadn't even broken a sweat or handled a gun. His suitcase was in the trunk. He'd already checked out of his motel, so now he was driving straight to the airport. He pulled out of the strip mall parking lot onto Simpson Boulevard and drove straight through the first intersection. Six blocks later, he took a left, circled around back onto Simpson, drove seven blocks to the next intersection and made a right turn onto Glendale Road. That's when he noticed the tail.

An old gray utility van with a painted-over name on the side was following three cars behind. Two men in the front. How many in the back? And whose were they? Stanley didn't know any hard guys, or he wouldn't have reached out to Zeb. Bryan slowed; the van slowed. He timed the next traffic light to rush through it on orange, but the van sped through on the red, barely avoiding a collision.

Off to the right, Bryan saw cars streaming out of the parking lot of a baseball park. Traffic was getting heavier and slower. Bryan wormed his way up through the traffic, trying to get as many cars in between himself and the van as possible. Up ahead, the left-turn lane was empty. At the last minute, he veered into the left lane, took the left onto Morris Drive, and then floored the Camry. He shot through the first stop sign, stepped on the brakes and slid through a right turn on the second sign, and was driving at normal residential speed through a rundown neighborhood of small houses at the edge of town when he saw the gray van behind him again. They must have planted a tracker on the Camry. This definitely wasn't Stanley.

He wasn't going to outrun them. His only chance was to ditch the car in a place that was so public and crowded that they might not try to kidnap him or kill him. Where had they come from? He'd been completely in the clear when he came to town. Was the counterfeiter making a play for his money? Or had the drug thugs from Springville managed to find him? Up ahead, on the right, was an abandoned gas station. Lots of cover there. The counterfeiter would want the money. He'd be safe in a crowd. Spanish Mike's guys, on the other hand, might just spray the crowd if they thought they could kill him. He needed to know who was tracking him.

Bryan pulled to a stop at the far side of the gas station, jumped out with his Glock in his hand, and scrambled for cover behind an old, rusty, bagged-ice freezer with a polar bear painted on the front. The van screeched to a stop by the broken-down gas pumps. Two Latino men jumped out, bulletproof vests on over their T-shirts, shot-guns in their hands. Bryan emptied his first magazine, firing low. The man wearing the green T-shirt fell to the pavement before he reached the cover of a gas pump. Bryan ducked. Buckshot punched into the freezer, obliterating the polar bear. Bryan scrambled backward, and then ran around behind the building into a junkyard of rusted car frames and broken equipment. There was no back door to the gas station.

Bryan ejected the empty magazine and inserted a fresh one. There was one guy left, the guy wearing the white T-shirt under his vest. Would he go for the money or come to kill him? And if so, which side of the building would he come from? A Lincoln Town Car with a crushed front end offered cover from both sides. Bryan shimmied under the Lincoln and waited. He heard the van start up. Was the guy leaving? The van careened around the corner of the gas station, plowing through debris until it came to a stop against a truck frame. Something heavy bounced off the Lincoln. Bryan had his answer. He stayed still, controlling his breathing, waiting for his chance. From under the Lincoln, he couldn't see the windshield of the van; he could only see the bottom of the driver's door. But that door didn't open. The passenger's door did.

Bryan slid around to get a view from the other side of the Lincoln. He could hear White T-shirt's footsteps. He thought he saw a glimpse of a leg, but it wasn't enough to shoot at. The shotgun boomed. Debris ricocheted up under the Lincoln, stinging Bryan's face and arm. "Stop wasting my time," a voice said in accented English. "You can't escape. I'll make it easy on you."

White T-shirt's footsteps seemed to be moving away. Bryan thought about the van. What was in it? A better gun than the Glock in his hand or the .38 in his ankle holster? Another shotgun, maybe? He slipped out from under the Lincoln, sprang up in a crouch, and ran. The shotgun boomed again. Buckshot smashed into a washing machine just to his right. He veered left, stooped behind the truck frame, and then rolled up into the van from the passenger's side. He got up on his hands and knees. Behind the front seats, the inside of the van was configured for carrying equipment and materials, but the space was empty. The shotgun boomed and buckshot tore into the side of the van. Bryan lay on the floor. The shotgun boomed again, and Bryan could see daylight through a ragged hole. He jumped up and fired four shots through the hole, angling down as he fired. Then he dropped to the floor, waiting for the next load of buckshot. He held his breath, listening as hard as he could for footfalls or any noise that would tell him what was happening, but he couldn't hear anything over the pounding of his pulse in his ears.

Finally, he rolled over onto his back, breathing slowly, waiting for his heart rate to come back down. Then he slipped out of the van from the opposite side of where the shots were fired, crept down the side of the van, and ran around to the front of the gas station. Green T-shirt was lying on the cracked concrete by the gas pumps. Bryan ran over to him, pointing his Glock as he ran, but Green T-shirt didn't move. He picked up Green T-shirt's shotgun and put his own pistol in his belt. Then he ran back around the building. White T-shirt was looking in the driver's side door of the van when Bryan came around the corner and fired at his legs. He fell backward, clutching his shotgun to his chest. Bryan rushed him. Before White T-shirt could bring his shotgun to bear, Bryan had the barrel of his own shotgun shoved into White T-shirt's neck. "Put it down."

White T-shirt lay the shotgun down, and Bryan kicked it away. Bryan knelt down beside him. "You're not walking away from here, but you're not leaking too bad."

White T-shirt gave him a prison-yard glare. "You are way too hard to kill."

Bryan smiled. "*Mi hermano*, let me tell you how this bullshit works in real life, and you can decide if you'd like to participate. Do you want to die here, now, or do you want to die somewhere else at a later date?"

"Somewhere else."

"Where's the tracker on my car?"

"Right rear wheel well."

"How long you been tracking me?"

"Found you at that bar."

"Where are the rest of you?"

"You know I can't tell you that."

"Come on, Spanish Mike wouldn't send just two of you. Where are you guys staying?"

He shook his head.

"Oh, well." Bryan stood up and pressed the end of the shotgun barrel against White T-shirt's forehead.

"Please, man."

Bryan shrugged. "I got to know. Do you want to live?"

"It's 611 Elm Avenue. Right off Washington."

"You got a phone?"

He nodded. "Right pocket."

Bryan dug the phone out of his pocket and input 9-1-1. "Abandoned gas station on Kendle Road out past Clancy. Gunshot victims." He set the phone down on White T-shirt's chest, picked up White T-shirt's shotgun and carried both shotguns to his car. The tracker was where he said. Bryan tossed it into the bagged-ice freezer before he put the shotguns in the trunk.

He sat down in the driver's seat and took a deep breath. He was worn out. He wanted to find a place to rest, but he knew that would be a mistake. He needed to keep moving if he was going to stay alive. He input the Elm Avenue address into the map app on his phone, turned around and drove back into town.

The streetlights were on by the time he found Elm Street. Six-eleven Elm was an interior row house in an old set of two-story row houses, eight across, each long ago painted and customized by the individual owners, now in various states of disrepair. Two tattooed men, obviously gang members, sat in a black Cadillac Escalade parked on the street. Three men with crew cuts sat on the porch of the exact address he'd been given, drinking beer and looking around as if they were waiting for someone.

He never would have expected Spanish Mike to devote so many out-of-town resources to killing him. Two more guys he could have dealt with, but five were too many to handle alone. Bryan drove to the nearest entrance ramp to the beltway and got off two exits later. He found a Dumpster behind a mom-and-pop grocery on a side street and pulled over. No one was in the alley. He popped the trunk, wiped off the shotguns and then his handguns, and tossed them all into the Dumpster. Then he got back on the beltway and drove to the airport.

At a nearby Sparkle Wash, he drove through the automatic car wash, and then vacuumed the interior and wiped it down for prints. He left the Camry in the airport long-term parking with the keys in it, glanced around carefully, and strolled into the terminal with his carry-on bag. The $19,750 in cash and the $7,500 in counterfeit from the Dugout job were in the bag. In his wallet was a notarized letter written by an attorney stating that he was a professional gambler who habitually carried large sums of money. Carrying that letter, he'd never had problems getting through security.

He sauntered up to the ticket counter. He was going to Chicago, where he'd decide on the best way to get to Cricket Bay. That way he'd leave no paper or electronic trail. He purchased his ticket and headed for the security checkpoint.

JENNY, one of Spanish Mike's people, a young bleached blonde wearing high-heeled boots, tight jeans, and a cream-colored V-neck sweater, trailed Bryan through the security checkpoint and down the main hallway, talking on her phone as she walked. "You were right. The grifter made it to the airport. Shaved off his beard."

She followed him through the food court, looked at a fashion magazine while he bought a bottle of water, and continued after him until he sat down in a chair at his gate. She got out her phone. "Buy a ticket to Chicago on United."

She sat in a chair on the other side of the gate, playing a game on her phone and watching him. The gate agent announced boarding for the Chicago flight. People began crowding toward the gate in the usual assortment of business and vacation wear. A woman came into the gate area who could have been her sister: same boots, same jeans, collared shirt instead of the sweater. She took a seat as if she were waiting for a different flight. After Bryan started down the boarding ramp, she strolled over to Jenny. "Here's your ticket."

"Thanks," Jenny said. "I'll call from Chicago."

"Someone will be waiting for you."

LATER, at Denison's house, Nicole, dressed for bed in a large white T-shirt, stood in the doorway to the kitchen watching Denison putter about. He'd been avoiding her all evening, and she'd been giving him his space, hoping he might eventually come to her to say something about what he was feeling, but he hadn't. While she stood there, he emptied the dishwasher, reloaded it, and wiped down the counters, all without acknowledging her presence.

"You coming to bed?" she asked.

He set the sponge on the edge of the sink. "I don't know if I can do this anymore."

"I know."

He turned and looked at her.

She continued. "Your mind is churning. You're trying to find the tiniest bit of hope to hang onto, and it's nowhere to be found. You've convinced yourself that no matter what happens now Bell will be hurt or killed. So you start looking for the moment when it all went wrong. Not the moment when those guys came in here. Not the moment when Fred Stein yelled at us at Jerry's Surf House. So when was it?"

He looked at the floor between them. "That morning I called you and asked you to come here."

"Because?"

"Because I was so broken and lonely and feeling sorry for myself."

She shook her head. "No. Because if that's the moment where everything comes off the rails, then it's all your fault."

He was sniffling and blinking, as if he were trying not to cry. She moved toward him. He stepped back against the sink and put up his hands to block her. She slowly took his hands and lowered them. "Don't run away. It's not your fault. You didn't do anything wrong. No one can handle what you're feeling alone." She put his hands on her hips.

"I can't."

"This isn't romance, James." She stood up on her tiptoes, kissed him gently, and then put her arms around him and rested her face on his chest. "You need comfort, Jimmy, and I need comfort too. Let's comfort each other. When everything is done, when Bell is back, then we can decide whether our relationship is a mistake. Okay?"

He let out a gigantic sigh. "Okay."

IN THE LIVING room of the rental house on Rainy Street, Kevin Johnson was sprawled out on a plaid armchair, and Chris Billings was lying on the sofa. Empty beer cans crowded the coffee table. Billings got out a cigarette.

"No smoking in the house," Johnson said.

"What?"

"I don't make the rules."

Billings sat up and laid the cigarette down on the coffee table. "So Fred is sure this is the crew that ripped him off?"

"Yeah. He's sure of that one girl, anyway."

"Didn't he say he thought that she was his girlfriend?"

"Yeah. What's your point?"

"So that means they fuck for work. How about if we see if the princess won't cooperate?"

Johnson laughed. "You wanting to piss off Rudy?"

"I'm not talking force. Couldn't hurt to ask."

Johnson glanced down the hall to the bedrooms. He lowered his voice. "Rudy said no tastes. We want Fred to think he's in charge. And we don't want to get in trouble with her crew. We want to get the money and go, not end up in a gunfight. Remember, we're going to make our real money screwing Fred."

"Okay, okay. It's just boring hanging around here. Looking for some way to pass the time."

"I like it boring. Boring means getting paid for doing nothing, as opposed to getting paid for being shot at."

"True enough."

"I'm turning in. You want the bed or the sofa?"

"I'll just stay here."

"You sure?"

"Yeah." Billings picked up the cigarette. "I'm going out on the porch."

Billings sat on the top step to the porch, lit the cigarette, and inhaled deeply. The night was quiet. There were only a few lights on in the other houses in this beach rental neighborhood, but it had been insane when he was here during spring break season. Drunk girls, half-naked in the middle of the day, screwing anything on two legs. If they passed out after, he stole their cash and credit cards. Win-win. Why couldn't it be the same thing now? The other guys were pussies. Of course, if he really did get $25,000, that would be something. But he didn't have it yet.

He went back into the house. Kevin had gone into the last bedroom. He looked at the sofa, and then he looked at the locked door to the faux basement. The princess was a hell of a looker. Probably a tiger in the sack. He smiled. It couldn't hurt to ask. He went into the kitchen and got two glasses and a bottle of vodka. Then he came back to the basement door, listened to make sure the other guys weren't moving around, and unlocked the door. The light was on. He pulled the door closed very quietly and started down the stairs.

"Stay away from me." The princess was standing in the middle of the basement with her arms crossed. The striped sundress she was wearing reminded him of wrapping paper.

Billings continued to the bottom of the stairs. "Relax, I'm not going to hurt you. Let's have a drink and get to know each other." He put the vodka and the glasses on the card table.

She backed toward the corner farthest from the camping cot. "Get out of here."

"Why play hard to get? We both know you fuck guys to make them easier to swindle. Just come on over here and have a seat." He pulled one of the folding chairs out from the card table, and poured vodka into the glasses. "It's party time. I'll pay if that's what it takes to change your mind. Just you and me. I won't tell the others."

She screamed.

Billings rushed across the basement, grabbed her shoulder, and clapped his hand over her mouth.

Johnson, Grissom, and Stein came charging down the stairs. "What the hell?" Stein yelled. "Get your hands off her."

Billings shrugged. "What? It's no big deal. I didn't hurt her."

"You heard him," Grissom said.

"I told you this was a stupid idea," Johnson said.

"Get out of here," Stein said.

Billings stomped up the stairs. "Fuck you. I didn't do anything."

"You okay, Princess?" Grissom asked.

She was backed up against the plywood wall, her arms folded across her chest. "Don't come any closer."

"What an asshole," Stein said. "One of us is going to have to watch the door all the time."

"I'll go first," Johnson said.

"Can I trust you?" Stein asked.

"He'll be fine," Grissom said.

"I'm really sorry about this, Princess," Stein said. "I really am. We're going to make sure you're safe." He turned to the others. "Let's get out of here. Bring the booze."

They started back up the stairs.

"That guy really work at the club?" Stein asked.

"We needed muscle," Grissom said. "Muscle comes with crazy."

"Wonderful," Stein said.

"If it all turns to mud, you'll be glad we've got him."

BELL DIDN'T MOVE until she heard the door lock. She slid down the wall to the concrete floor, sat with her knees pulled up to her chest and her hands over her face, and sobbed. Mr. White was crazy. He would have raped her for sure. What if the others weren't here next time? What if they changed their minds? She dried her face on her dress and got to her feet. What could she use to defend herself? Besides the table and chairs and the cot, all there was in the room was a broom and dustpan. She tiptoed up the stairs and tried to wedge the dustpan under the door, but it wouldn't stick. She crept back down. She stood in the middle of the room and swung the broom around, holding the bristles down, trying to find the best grip to have the most force if she needed to use it as a club. Who was she kidding? She was completely at their mercy.

She took another look around the room. There was nothing sharp or pointed laying anywhere—no scrap wood, no screwdriver. Not even a pencil. Mr. White had acted like having sex with all of them would be nothing to her. Why? Because he thought she was part of Nicole's gang? Because he thought that Nicole used sex to manipulate men? She lay down on the cot, clutching the broom handle to her body. Is that what Nicole was really like? Is that how Nicole controlled her dad? She'd been such a fool to believe her. What had Nicole convinced her dad of in the last two months? What was she telling him right now?

10

THE GUNFIGHTER

Bryan walked into the crowd surrounding his departure gate. He'd spent the night sleeping in O'Hare International Airport in Chicago. It was the one place in the city where he knew no one could be gunning for him. The plane to Atlanta was going to be full. All the chairs in the waiting area were taken. A baby was crying. The screen above the counter by the door showed a standby list of six people. He'd had to buy a first-class ticket to get a seat, but Denison was going to pay for it. Twenty minutes until boarding. He walked down the hall to an empty gate where no one would overhear him and made a phone call to Zeb.

"Hey, brother, I've got some trouble dogging me, but I don't think they know about that little job you put me on."

"Okay. Should I warn Stanley?"

"No, he might overreact. I'll keep you posted."

"Okay."

"I am a little concerned about the discretion of the money guy you sent me to."

"How's that?"

"He was the only guy who knew who I was and saw my car."

"I'll see what I can find out."

"Thanks."

"You still need that gunslinger?"

"All taken care of."

"If it was my guy who screwed you, I'll take care of it."

"I expected as much."

Bryan went into the men's room, splashed water in his face, and examined himself in the mirror. He was exhausted, but he looked pretty good considering the day he'd had. He strolled back down to his gate. The counterfeiter had to have sold him out. There was no way Spanish Mike's people just fell on him. This airplane trip would make a fresh start. He'd received a text that Billy had come through. With any luck, they'd be able to deal with Stein's crew without getting Bell killed. The crowd at his gate was even larger now. Shit. The screen above the counter said that the flight was delayed. He walked down the hall and called Nicole. "Hey, honey."

"Bryan, where are you?"

"I'm in Chicago."

"When are you going to get here?"

"My flight's delayed."

"I thought you'd be here this morning."

"I'm moving as fast as I can." He explained what happened.

"Spanish Mike's guys found you? How?"

"Maybe the money guy. I think I've really lost them this time. I've been buying my airline tickets flight by flight, so I'll get to Atlanta and then buy the ticket to Cricket Bay. It slows me down, but it's better than bringing trouble with me. Keep me posted of any problems."

JENNY SAT in a chair near the windows at the gate, her hair in a loose ponytail. She was on standby, and she knew this flight was going to Atlanta, but she didn't know if that was the grifter's final destination. She watched him read the screen over the counter and show his frustration. Did he have a tight connection? She got out her phone. "Hey, Spanish, he's going to Atlanta on Delta. Plane's delayed—I'm on standby."

"Okay, we'll get someone in the airport."

STEIN KNOCKED on the basement door before he started down the stairs with a plate of donuts and a mug of coffee. The princess was standing by the cot in her wrinkled sundress with the broomstick in her hands as if she meant business.

"Is it time to go?"

"Not yet. I'm going to call Denison in about an hour."

Stein set the coffee and donuts on the card table and backed away. "Have something to eat. At least drink some coffee. You'll feel better."

The princess moved slowly toward the table, the broom handle leaning on her right shoulder, watching for any movement from Stein. When she got to the table, she picked the mug up with her left hand, still watching Stein, and took a tentative sip.

Stein held his hands up in surrender mode. "I'm not going to hurt you."

"Why should I believe you?"

"You think I changed my mind since last night?"

"The other guy, Mr. White—"

"Sorry about that. I really am. Sit down. He isn't even in the house right now."

She kept standing.

"You mind if I sit down?" He sat down on the stairs. "I can see now that you're not a grifter, Princess. What do you do?"

The princess watched him suspiciously. "Do?"

"Yeah."

"I'm a college professor."

"Really? What do you teach?"

"Art history."

"I took one of those classes as an elective."

The princess set the coffee mug down and picked up a glazed donut.

Stein continued. "You know your girlfriend is a professional thief?"

"She's not my friend."

"Oh, so you're sticking to her story that she's conning Denison?"

"My dad hasn't given her any money, and he's not going to."

"Princess, please, with her kind, there's always a scam. You better keep an eye on your bank account. Once upon a time she was my girl-friend. I ended up in jail, and she ended up with my money."

"And that's the money you want back?"

"Yeah, that's right. That's the money I want back. My money."

"Which you stole from someone else."

"Please. That corporation was screwing everybody in sight. I earned that money. It was mine. And she stole it from me. She didn't give it to the police. She took that money, and my family was broke. I was in jail."

"I don't see how taking my dad's money makes you even with her."

"Once your dad got involved with her, it wasn't his money."

SHORTLY AFTER 9:00 A.M., Nicole and Denison stood in the kitchen drinking coffee while they waited for Stein to call. Denison's eyes were red-rimmed. He'd been up most of the night. He had already spoken to Cory Davids at the bank. They were still gathering the money, so his only hope of getting Bell back this morning had evaporated. And even though Nicole had finally gotten him to lie down before dawn, Bell's kidnapping still hung between them, so she hadn't been able to get him to settle, and he'd tossed and turned until he finally got up.

She felt sorry for him, sorry that she had brought this trouble to his door, but she couldn't let her emotions cloud the decisions she had to make. She had to remain clear-headed. The more time passed, the more paranoid Stein was going to become, the less controllable his partners would be, and the more dangerous the situation became. Every choice could be life or death for Bell.

"This is so messed up," Denison said.

"Focus," Nicole said. "Stein is going to call in a few minutes. You don't know how he's going to take the news. Is he going to pretend to be angry or is he going to be angry? Is he going to threaten to hurt Bell or is he going to hurt her? You've got to keep him believing that you know he's in charge."

Denison's eyes teared up. "Christ, this is the one time having money is supposed to make all the difference." He palmed the tears out of his eyes.

Nicole squeezed his arm. "You can do this, James. You can do this."

The phone on the kitchen counter rang.

"Have you got the money?" Stein asked.

"The bank still hasn't assembled it. They're waiting for one more delivery. It might not happen today. As soon as they have the money, they're supposed to call me."

"What kind of bullshit is this? You think I won't hurt her?"

"I'm not making this up. I want my daughter back. If there was any way I could get my hands on the money, I'd be bringing it to you right now."

"You better make this happen fast or I won't be responsible for what happens to the princess."

"I could give you what they've collected."

"I want the entire one hundred thousand. Make it happen."

"Can I talk to her?"

"No." The line went dead.

Denison hung up the phone.

"You did good," Nicole said.

"I should call the police."

"We've been over this. They can't help. We've got a pretty good idea where she is. We're going to rescue her and make sure these guys never bother you again."

"What if Bryan and the other guy don't get here in time?"

She took his hand. "Jimmy, I'm going to be honest with you. It's not what you want to hear, but it's the truth. We don't have any control over how those guys act. The worst thing you can think of, if those guys are capable of it, they're already doing it. They're not going to wait."

The color drained from Denison's face. "But he said..."

She shook her head. "If they're monsters, they're going to act like monsters. If they're professionals, they'll act professional. If they're amateurs, they'll act like amateurs. We've got no control over that. What we do have control over is how we respond."

Denison lurched across to the sink and threw up. Nicole went after him, handed him a paper towel, and filled a glass from the tap. She talked to him like to a sick child. "Rinse your mouth." He took the glass. "You're going to be okay, Jimmy. You're going to be okay. Bell is going to be okay. We're going to get her back."

She led him back to a stool at the kitchen island. "Bryan and the hired guy are going to get here. We're going to find the bad guys and deal with them. We're going to be much more likely to save Bell than the police are because we're going to do whatever it takes, not just what the law allows. Do you understand?"

"My God, Nicki, if anything happens to her..."

"I know, Jimmy, I know. Do you need a drink?"

He shook his head. "That would be betraying Bell."

"James, you're a mess. You need to be in control of your emotions if you're going to help." She poured two fingers of whiskey into a glass and pushed it toward him.

"What do we do now?"

"We work our plan. The hired gun is supposed to get here at one o'clock."

STEIN ENDED the phone call and tried to avoid looking at the others. They were standing around him in the living room of the little house on Rainy Street, where they'd been listening to his side of the conversation. The place was already a pigsty. Beer cans and fast-food wrappers were strewn over the counters. An empty pizza box sat next to a half-empty donut box. Stein pulled the chip from his burner phone.

"Well?" Grissom asked.

"You heard. The bank is still putting the money together."

"How much longer?"

"Might not be until tomorrow."

"Another day?" Johnson said. He ran his hand back through his Afro.

"That's a load of crap," Billings said. "Let's smack her around a little, just to raise up a few bruises, send him a picture to get him motivated."

"No way," Stein said.

"I'm not talking about actually hurting her."

"Chris, you're going to stay away from the girl," Grissom said.

"You guys don't know what you're doing."

Grissom picked up his pistol from the dining room table. "I've had enough of your shit. You can get back on the team or you can leave."

Billings looked from Grissom to Johnson.

"Don't look at Kevin," Grissom said. "He's not going to give up a payday just because you won't settle down."

Johnson shrugged. "Sorry, man."

Billings held up his hands. "Rudy, I'm not wanting any trouble. I was just making a suggestion."

"You're not helping."

"Maybe Denison can get the rest of the money somewhere else. Maybe he's got something he could sell. That's all I'm saying."

Stein cut in. "We've got a plan. We wait 'til tomorrow if we have to."

Grissom nodded. "We're sticking with the plan."

"Okay," Billings said.

"But if we don't have the money by then, we'll have to change our game," Grissom said.

"Now you're talking."

Grissom pointed his free hand at Billings. "But until tomorrow, we're not doing a fucking thing."

"Okay."

"Does that work for you, Fred?"

Stein nodded. "That's fine with me. They're going to get the money. Denison wants the princess back."

"But now we've got to babysit her all day," Johnson said.

"I promise I won't touch her," Billings said.

"Why should we trust you?" Stein asked.

"I was drunk. I was willing to pay. I didn't think she would mind, okay?"

"You don't inspire confidence."

"Fuck you." Billings stormed out the front door.

Johnson shook his head. "We're going to have to watch him."

"He won't try anything while we're all awake," Grissom said.

"Maybe we'll get the money before the end of the day," Stein said.

ONCE NICOLE GOT on the ramp to the Jonas Grey Airport the traffic was light. She drove the Explorer past the arrivals gate and the baggage claim entrance and pulled into the short-term parking deck across the street. Only a few people were unloading luggage onto the sidewalk. She walked quickly into the terminal and down the hall to the arrivals passageway next to the security checkpoint. Billy had texted a picture of the gunslinger: red-gray hair, weathered face, two-day beard, jeans and hoody—a hard man going by the name Cohen. A crowd from a just-landed plane passed through the arrivals door-way. Nicole spotted her man and held her hand up. Cohen came over to her, a carryon over his shoulder. He was taller than she thought he would be. She stuck out her hand.

Cohen frowned. "Where's your old man?"

"He gets here later."

"I've never worked for a woman before."

"Is that a problem?"

"Billy tells me you're more than a pretty face, so we'll see how it goes."

They walked out of the terminal and across to the parking deck. "You come well recommended," Nicole continued.

"Whatever that means. You don't get to know anything about me.

We're not at summer camp. We're just doing some killing together. You got the guns?"

"We pick them up later."

"Targets here?"

"Yeah. Hoping to deal with them this evening."

"Fill me in on the details."

Nicole explained what they knew so far.

"Well, you know my scale. I don't want any bitching if I kill more than you planned on."

"Right now, I'm not concerned about killing too few, I'm concerned about not killing them fast enough."

Neither spoke on the way back to the beach house. Denison was standing at the kitchen island drinking a glass of wine when Nicole and Cohen came in. "This is Cohen," she said. "And this is my boyfriend James. It's his daughter that's been kidnapped."

Cohen gave Denison an appraising look. "Civilian."

"Yeah," Nicole said. "He's not in the game. Do you want a drink?"

"Not now."

"Something to eat?"

"I need a place to sleep."

"Let's put him in the north bedroom," Denison said.

Nicole led Cohen down the hall to the bedroom. He dropped his carryon onto the floor by the door. "Wake me when you need me," he said.

When she returned to the kitchen, Denison handed her a glass of wine. "That guy looks like a psychopath."

"But he's our psychopath, and he works for ten thousand dollars a gunfight. Which reminds me, you need to get a doctor lined up."

"What for?"

"After we rescue Bell, we can't take her to the emergency room. Too many questions. She's going to need to be checked out. She may need a tranquilizer."

"She's going to need a doctor?"

"Just planning for the worst. Maybe Bell will be fine, and one of us will be shot up."

"You aren't kidding, are you? This is your plan?"

"You're going to drive yourself crazy if you think too hard about what might happen. You've got a spare tire and a jack in your car, don't you? It's there even though you probably won't need it. When you're driving, you're not thinking that you're going to get a flat, are you? Think about it like that. Can you line up a doctor?"

"I'll take care of it."

TWO HOURS LATER, Nicole and Cohen pulled out of Denison's driveway in the Explorer. It was a beautiful afternoon, full sun with a light breeze. Seagulls glided back and forth over the beach, and the noises of the vacationers mixed with the sounds of the waves. Cohen had his hood up. "Where are we going?"

"Can you Google 2011 Seagull Way?"

Cohen found the address on his phone. "Looks like it's by the public docks."

Nicole pulled out onto Lighthouse Boulevard. Traffic was light, even though the beaches were crowded. They rode in silence until Nicole turned onto the access road to the Cricket Bay Marina.

"So there are four guys holding the girl?" Cohen asked.

"Yeah. And she's not a kid. She's a grown woman."

"So why not just pay?"

"We'd be happy to if we thought we could trust them. But maybe they've already fucked her up. Best case scenario, they can't just let us walk. We've seen them. If we're criminals, we want payback. If we're not, we could go to the police. You know as well as I do that's what they're going to be thinking about when we bring them the money. If just one of them is an asshole or has a quick temper..."

"Yeah, they screwed up from the get-go. Should have worn masks. Kidnapping...that's real shit work. Take the next left around the sheet-metal warehouse."

Nicole followed the asphalt around past a Dumpster. Small motorboats and sailboats on their trailers were parked in rows along the edge of the shore near the boat ramp. A dented red Ford pickup truck with a white camper top was parked behind the warehouse. Nicole stopped twenty feet away and got out of the SUV. A small, dark-skinned man wearing jeans, work boots, and an unbuttoned, long-sleeved shirt got out of the truck. "Why are you here?"

"Billy sent me."

The man waved for Nicole to pull up. Nicole got back in the Explorer. Cohen looked at her. "What you think?"

"Wish I had a gun."

The man was waiting at the tailgate of the truck when Nicole pulled up beside him. "What you got for me?"

"Full package." The man lowered the tailgate. Three large cases were in the bed of the truck. He pulled the closest one onto the tailgate and opened it. A Kevlar vest was strapped inside the lid. A Glock pistol, an MP5K submachine gun, boxes of ammunition, and several extra magazines sat in impressions in a foam board.

Nicole nodded approvingly. "This is the good stuff."

"Billy said to hook you up; I hook you up."

Nicole reached for the Glock. The man pushed her hand away. "What you do once the cases are in your car doesn't concern me, but not here."

"Fair enough. All three the same?"

The man nodded.

"What's the damage?"

"Your arrangement is with Billy. You pay him."

"Okay."

They transferred the cases to the back of the Explorer. The truck drove away. "Let's find a spot to have another look," Nicole said.

They left the marina and drove along the shore to a city park access point across the boulevard from the beach. No one was parked in the gravel lot. They pulled into a spot at the far corner away from the restrooms and the path leading to the picnic tables and playground equipment. "See any cameras?" she asked.

"No."

They opened the liftback. The contents of all three cases were the same. They took two of the pistols, filled the magazines and seated them. Cohen felt the weight of the loaded gun in his hand. "The day's getting better already."

A car pulled into the parking lot. A middle-aged woman wearing a straw hat and a long, loose dress got out with her German shepherd and started down the path. Nicole closed the liftback. She and Cohen got back into the front. "When's Bryan supposed to get here?" Cohen asked.

"I'm not sure."

"But everything else is in place?"

"Yeah. We just need Bryan to help even up the odds."

Back at the beach house they unloaded the cases in the garage and carried them through to the kitchen. Denison came into the room, Bell's laptop in his hand. "The phone still at the house?" Nicole asked.

"It's moving around town," Denison said. "What you got here?"

Nicole lifted one of the cases on to the island and opened it.

"Wow," Denison said. "Are those automatic weapons? Where did you get them?"

"Bryan reached out to a friend." She pointed to the computer. "You're going to drive yourself crazy."

"I know. I just can't help myself. Can't focus, and I need something to do."

"Did you line up the doctor?"

"All taken care of."

"You want to help?" Cohen asked. "You ever been fingerprinted?"

"No."

"All the extra magazines need to be filled. You know how to do it?" Cohen picked up an MP5K magazine, opened a box of cartridges, and inserted one into the magazine. "See? It's easy. Just like that."

"Okay," Denison said.

"Might seem like grunt work, but it's essential. All the mags in all three cases."

"Got you."

BRYAN STEPPED off the plane train in the Hartsfield-Jackson International Airport and went up the escalator into his concourse. Even though he'd slept all the way from Chicago in a comfortable first-class seat, he still felt groggy. He turned toward the Caffeination Coffee Shop located just before the moving sidewalk. As he walked, he took out his phone and called Nicole. "Hey, baby."

"Bryan? Where are you?"

"I'm in Atlanta. My flight was delayed three hours. Mechanical problems."

"When will you get here?"

"If there're no delays, ten or eleven o'clock."

"That late?"

"What's the gunslinger like?"

"Billy came through. He's the real deal. And the gear is top shelf."

"Billy's probably wanting more of our business. And he may get it if it turns out Zeb's guy was an asshole."

"Should we wait for you?"

"I know waiting's a bitch, but we're only going to get one chance to surprise them. We need overwhelming force if we're going to have any chance at all. Have you got the money yet?"

"No. Definitely tomorrow."

"Denison doing any better?"

"He's adjusting."

"Good. Don't let him talk you into giving him a gun."

"I know."

"I'm serious."

"I know."

"He'll shoot himself or one of you."

"I'm not going to give him a gun."

"Good. I'll be there just a soon as I can, and then we'll get this sorted out."

SPANISH MIKE'S ATLANTA PERSON, a middle-aged woman wearing khaki pants and a zip-up jacket, stood next to a Burrito Time restaurant pretending to read the menu while she watched Bryan at the Caffeination Coffee Shop. She got out her phone. "Found your guy."

"You sure?" Jenny asked.

"It's definitely him."

"Great. Follow him to his gate and call me back."

NICOLE SET her phone down on the counter. She knew that Bryan was right, but she was worried about Bell. It was the second day. Was she bound and gagged in a closet? Locked in a room? Guys like these often lacked impulse control. Bell wasn't the kind of woman who would submit. If they decided to party her out while they waited, how hard would she fight back? Would they be willing to beat her down to have sex on her?

Cohen and Denison stopped filling magazines. "Well?" Denison asked.

"Bryan's still in Atlanta. Won't get here until late."

Cohen nodded. "So what's the plan?"

"Let's go get Bell," Denison said. "There's three of us. We've got machine guns and bulletproof vests."

Cohen shook his head. "When was the last time you were at the gun range?"

"I know how to fire a gun."

"This isn't firing a gun. This is hot work that's got to be done with a cool head. You get yourself killed, shame on you. You get me killed, shame on me."

"Cohen's right," Nicole said. "You're no gunfighter. We're better off without you in the mix."

"You're not leaving me here. She's my daughter. I need to be there."

"If you come, you've got to stay in the car. No matter what you hear, no matter what you see, you can't get out. You've got to wait for the all-clear."

"I can do that."

"You think you can do that," Cohen said. "You run up in the mix and get shot, you probably won't live long enough for me to say I told you so."

"I promise. I'll stay in the car. You've got my word."

Nicole turned to Cohen. "You think we can do it? There's four of them maximum."

"You sure?"

She nodded. "Fred Stein is no gunman, but Acne Scars looks like a tough guy. And Mr. Black and Mr. White look like they follow orders and don't back down."

"So it's three and a half?"

"Yeah," she said.

"It's definitely doable."

Nicole heard Bryan's voice in the back of her mind. He was right. They would only get one chance to surprise Stein's crew. Waiting for him was the smart move. There was no doubt about it. But how long would they have to wait? What if Bryan's flight had another delay? What if Bell was hurt and needed medical attention right now? What if they hadn't raped her yet, but raped her tonight while she and Cohen were still waiting for Bryan? Cohen was a professional. A hard guy. Him and the element of surprise. It was worth the risk.

"Okay, we hit that house just after dark," Nicole said. "If we're lucky, she's there. If not, we'll have to get one of those guys to tell us where she is."

"What if they won't talk?" Denison asked.

"They'll talk. This isn't the movie of the week. We're going to bring Bell home tonight."

11

RAINY STREET

Nicole, Cohen, and Denison sat in the dark in a stolen Suburban on the street one block up from the kidnappers' safe house on Rainy Street. They were dressed in dark clothing and wearing the Kevlar vests. Nicole and Cohen had the Glocks holstered at their hips and the MP5Ks slung from their shoulders. They wore black ball caps with FBI printed across the front in yellow just in case they attracted the attention of any neighbors. The blue minivan, a Toyota Corolla, and a Jeep crowded the driveway. The street was quiet. There were lights on in about a quarter of the houses, but no one was on the street.

Nicole turned in her seat to look at both Cohen and Denison. "Okay, we've got the front door into the living room, back door into the kitchen, bedrooms and bathroom on the left from the front."

Cohen and Denison nodded.

"There may be as many as four hostiles. Probably are, judging from the number of vehicles. Cohen and I will go in the front and back—"

"I'll hit the front," Cohen said.

Nicole pointed at Denison. "And you're going to wait here until we bring Bell out."

"Okay."

Nicole turned to Cohen. "You ready?"

"Anyone points a gun, I'm killing everyone."

"Except the woman."

"Except the woman."

"Let's get this done."

They crept up to the house and then split up. Cohen counted to ten, ran up the stairs to the porch, and kicked in the front door. As the door flew open, Mr. White sprang up from the sofa firing a revolver and then dove over the back of the sofa; Stein reached for a pistol on the coffee table. Cohen shot him three times in the chest before he could get to his feet. Mr. White slithered through the doorway into the hall. In the kitchen, Mr. Black scrambled for a shotgun on the counter.

Just then, Nicole kicked in the back door. She pulled the trigger on the MP5K, and Mr. Black fell in a heap. She looked at Cohen. He nodded. They moved into the hall. There were four doors, all closed. Nicole reached for the nearest doorknob on her right. Locked. Cohen put his right hand on Nicole's left shoulder. Nicole raised up her machine gun and nodded. Cohen kicked in the door with a martial arts side kick. The door slammed open just as a shotgun blast cut a hole through it. Nicole fired as the door swung back. The MP5K spat slugs through the half-open door. Now everything was silent. Nicole glanced into the room. Acne Scars lay in the bathtub tangled up with the shower curtain. She whispered, "That's three. And still no Bell. The only one of them left is Mr. White."

Cohen tried the door on the left. It was unlocked. He gave it a gentle push. Down the stairs, he saw Mr. White standing behind a tall redhead, his revolver pushed into her neck, his finger on the trigger. "Move down the hall to the bedrooms. You go toward the kitchen, she's dead."

Nicole tiptoed back down the hall. She had to save Bell. Nothing else mattered. She was only going to get one chance. She couldn't let Mr. White take her. His partners were dead, and he'd want revenge. James was counting on her. She'd promised him she'd rescue her.

She positioned herself to one side of the kitchen doorway and stood completely still, crouched and ready to strike.

Cohen stepped out of the doorway and toward the bedrooms. Mr. White moved slowly up the stairs, pushing Bell ahead of him. She was trembling and gasping softly, as if she were too afraid to sob. "Keep moving."

Mr. White and Bell came out of the stairwell. "Where's your partner?"

"She got shot," Cohen said.

"I'm not stupid enough to try to take your guns. You can shoot me, but she's still going to die. Back up into the bedroom."

Cohen backed down the hall and went into one of the bedrooms. Mr. White moved more quickly now, pulling Bell down the hall toward the kitchen. Just as he came through the doorway, Nicole sprang on him, grabbed his gun with both hands, and snatched it away from Bell's neck. The revolver went off. Bell screamed. They all banged into the refrigerator, Nicole shoving herself between Bell and Mr. White as they struggled over the revolver.

"Run," she yelled.

Bell stumbled backward and then turned and ran through the chaos in the living room and out onto the porch, where Denison was running up the steps. "Bell! I'm here! I'm here!"

Bell looked around, disoriented and confused. "Dad?"

He pulled her into his arms. "Come with me."

In the kitchen, Nicole and Mr. White were grappling, banging into the counter and the table, each trying to bring the gun to bear on the other. Nicole tried to head-butt him, but her feet slipped in Mr. Black's blood, and she lost her grip on the revolver. She reached for her Glock as she fell. Mr. White shot her twice in the vest. She felt her ribs crack. He kicked her in the head. She blacked out. Mr. White took her submachine gun in one hand, grabbed her by the hair and dragged her through the living room and out onto the porch. Cohen was waiting out in the front yard, his feet planted on the sidewalk, his machine gun ready.

"It's still the same standoff," Mr. White said. "You can kill me, if you don't mind losing her. Move back."

Cohen stepped back into the yard.

"Get up." Mr. White, his hand still tangled in Nicole's hair, pulled her to her feet. She gasped, holding her side. Mr. White pulled her down the steps and across the yard to the Jeep. Police sirens wailed in the distance.

"We can still make a deal," Cohen said.

"We'll see," Mr. White said. He forced Nicole into the Jeep from the driver's side, and kept the machine gun pressed into her side as he backed out of the driveway.

Denison came running from the Suburban as the Jeep sped off. "Chase them down?"

Cohen shook his head. "Cops are coming. We need to get your daughter home and make a new plan."

BELL, quietly sobbing, lay on the sofa in the den curled up in a ball. Denison knelt next to her, holding her hand. The doctor, a young south Asian woman wearing olive-colored slacks and a baby blue, long-sleeve button-up shirt, stood nearby. "Physically, your daughter is fine, Mr. Denison. I gave her a sedative. She should fall asleep momentarily. I can recommend some therapists."

"Dad, Dad," Bell murmured. "She pushed in front of me, told me to run. We've got to help her, Dad."

Denison squeezed her hand. He blinked away his tears and swallowed hard. "Did they hurt you?"

"The bad guy wanted to, but the others wouldn't let him."

"The bad guy?"

"Mr. White."

He kissed her forehead. He turned to the doctor. "Can you stay the night?"

"Of course."

He went into the kitchen, where Cohen sat at the island drinking a beer. "My God, what are we going to do?"

"That's above my pay grade."

"Maybe it's time for the police."

Cohen shook his head. "That's the one thing we can't do. We left three dead retrieving your daughter. This is our private fiasco. Besides, we don't know where they are. All the cops can do is arrest us."

"We've got to do something."

"We are doing something. We're waiting for Bryan. He's the one who's going to have to sort this out."

TWO HOURS later Bryan was in a rented Nissan Sentra driving away from the Jonas Grey Airport in Cricket Bay. The night sky was clear, and the traffic was light. He's been trying to call Nicole ever since he had landed, but she wasn't picking up, and he wasn't going to leave a message. He was tired from traveling, paranoid from being chased by Spanish Mike's people, and hoping, just hoping, that things here weren't as bad as Nicole's silence seemed to suggest.

ON THE SIDEWALK in front of the terminal, a skinny woman wearing discount-store fashion, her face ruined by drugs and alcohol, was talking on her phone. "That's right, Jenny. It was him for sure. He got away before I could get to my car."

"He got away? Is that what I'm paying you for?"

"I'm sorry. I really am. I got his license plate, though."

"You sure?"

"Yeah. It's a rental."

"Give me the plate number."

AS BRYAN PULLED into Denison's driveway, he noted the security features on the house: yard lights, window alarms, but nothing to provide protection if someone wanted in and could beat the police response time. He rang the doorbell. Denison answered the door.

"You look like shit," Bryan said. "Got here as soon as I could. I've been trying to call Nicole. Where is she?"

Denison stammered. "I don't know how to tell you this..."

Bryan pushed past him. "Where is she?" He moved down the hall-way, saw the doctor and Bell in the den, and stopped in the kitchen. "You must be the gunfighter."

Cohen nodded. His face was set, and he had his hand on the butt of his holstered pistol.

"Where's Nicole?"

Cohen filled him in. Bryan turned to Denison. "So we got your daughter back in mint condition, except for a few scuffs. Narrowed them down from four to one. But we don't know where the last guy took her."

"And Bell says this guy Mr. White is the bad one," Denison said.

"You should have waited for me."

"We thought we could take them."

"We? We? You don't know a thing about this kind of work."

"She thought we could take them."

"And she thought wrong."

"I can get the money in the morning."

"God damn it."

He glanced at Cohen. His pistol was loose in his holster. "You can relax, soldier. I'm not blaming you."

"You sure about that?"

"Yeah. It was just a bad break. You did your job."

"You still need my services?"

Bryan nodded. "Oh, yeah. I'm definitely going to need your help. We've still got some killing ahead of us."

"What are you going to do?" Denison asked.

"That bastard doesn't know about me. We're going to give him a chance to settle so that we have a place to find, then we're going to get Nicole back, and I'm going to murder that asshole."

"How can you be sure she isn't already dead?"

"Nicole is too valuable to kill. He may be pissed about his buddies, but he still wants the money. As long as he thinks he can get the cash, he's going to keep her alive. Count on it."

BILLINGS STOOD in the dark by the front door to the motel room. Outside, the parking lot was quiet. In the light from the bathroom, he could see Nicole lying face-down on the king-size bed, her mouth gagged with a washcloth and duct tape, her arms tied behind her back, and her knees taped together. He set her phone down on the scratched-up table by the door next to the MP5K and the Glock. The Kevlar vest lay on the floor. He could see her eyes watching him, trying to figure him out. What a clusterfuck. Rudy and Kevin dead. That house was a death trap. He barely got out of there alive. This was her doing, and she was going to pay. He walked by her into the bathroom, urinated, washed his hands, and came back out into the room.

"You fucked up. He got the princess, but I got you. You better hope they're willing to trade a hundred thousand dollars for your skanky ass."

He dragged her off the edge of the bed, pulled out his pocketknife, and cut the duct tape binding her knees. "But the bank doesn't open 'til morning, so we've got all night for you to tell me about your friends, particularly the big bastard who did the killing." He cut through her belt and tossed his knife onto the night table. "First we're going to get to know each other a little better. You owe me that much. You going to spread your legs and pretend that you like it?"

She drove her boots into the carpet and sprang up, banging her shoulder into his chest. He staggered back. She turned to face him, pivoted on her left foot to swing with her right, but he stepped out of range, and her momentum spun her around. He grabbed her from behind. She kicked and writhed. He punched her in her cracked ribs. She groaned through her gag and fell limp. He tossed her face down onto the bed and jerked her pants down. She turned her head to try to look at him. He pushed down hard in the middle of her back. "Quit struggling. This isn't your first time."

12

GANGBANGERS

The next morning, the gunfight at the rental house was on all the local TV news shows. Three men dead, the house riddled with bullet holes. The gang taskforce was in charge of the investigation. No leads. Denison and Bell were still asleep when Bryan and Cohen left in the white Sentra, tracking Nicole's phone. It appeared to be moving away from the White Sands Motel when the signal died. They rolled into the motel's potholed parking lot. The motel was a single strip of rooms built in the 1960s, peeling paint and missing screens, located next to a pool hall and a whiskey bar. The parking lot was empty. Bryan got out of the car and went into the office. The window air conditioner whirred as if the fan blades were bent. An elderly woman wearing a cardigan sweater sat at a stool behind the wire mesh-enclosed counter, watching a cable news show. "Were you working last night?"

"Got here at seven a.m." Her dentures clicked as she talked.

"How could I get ahold of the night guy?"

She studied his face. "You know him?"

"I just need some information." He pushed a twenty-dollar bill through the slot in the mesh.

She took the twenty. "He'll be here at seven tonight."

"No address?"

She shook her head.

Bryan drove out onto the boulevard and turned onto Trion Drive. Cohen looked in his side mirror and then over his shoulder. "I think we've got a tail. Check out the old Lincoln."

Bryan glanced in the rearview mirror. A yellow Lincoln with tinted windows was two cars behind. Bryan took a right turn. The Lincoln took a right turn. Bryan took a left. The Lincoln took a left. The light at the approaching intersection was green. Bryan got in the left turn lane. When the light turned yellow, he swerved out of the turn lane and drove through the intersection, causing the car behind him to slam on the brakes and honk its horn. Cohen looked over his shoulder. "He's boxed in the left turn lane."

Bryan sped up, took the next left turn, and then another quick left.

"What are you doing?" Cohen asked.

"Trying to come up in back of them so we can find out who they are." He sped through two residential intersections, took another left, and came back out on Trion Drive. Up ahead, the Lincoln was stopped at a traffic light.

"Good driving."

"Yeah, as long as I don't lose them."

The Lincoln circled around a few times, as if it were trying to find them, and then took an entrance ramp onto the beltway. Three exits down, the Lincoln got off the beltway and pulled into the Weekender Motel, a truck driver's motel just south of the interchange. Groups of men dressed in jeans and work boots sat on folding chairs in front of the motel room doors drinking from bottles in sacks. "New players," Bryan said.

"They were following you."

"I had some guys after me before I got here. Hard to believe it's them, but they certainly are persistent."

"You going to add them to my list?"

"One problem at a time. Nicole's our priority."

Bryan pulled into the motel and stopped behind a parked tractor-trailer rig. "See which room they go in."

Cohen hopped out and peeked around the trailer. The Lincoln slipped into a parking spot about halfway down the lot. Four Latinos piled out and went into room 179. Cohen watched the door shut before he went back to the Sentra.

"Hard guys. Definite trouble."

"They must have seen me rent the car, but they didn't follow us to Denison's or we'd have met them there. Time to change cars."

They returned the Sentra to the Enterprise car rental at the airport. Then they walked over to the long-term parking section of the parking deck and waited. A middle-aged man in a sports coat, overnight bag on one shoulder, parked a Toyota Highlander. Short trip. One or two days, tops. A black woman in a pantsuit, one rolling suitcase that would fit in the overhead compartment, parked a mini-van. Maybe three or four days. Then a couple wearing Eddie Bauer travel clothes parked a Honda CR-V and unloaded three suitcases. "They won't be back this week," Bryan said.

Bryan broke into the driver's side, hotwired the ignition, and opened the passenger's door.

"Pretty quick," Cohen said.

"Practice makes perfect."

They drove back to Denison's with the windows open, the salt air blowing through the car, Cohen tapping his foot, and Bryan humming to himself. Finally Cohen spoke. "This time's going to be harder."

Bryan nodded.

"No element of surprise."

"Yep."

"We going to wait for night?"

Bryan turned onto Lighthouse Boulevard. "I'm going to try to put the gangsters into the mix."

Cohen shifted in his seat so that he could concentrate on Bryan's face. "How's that?"

"Asshole isn't expecting them."

"Okay, but how are you going to get them to cooperate? They want to kill you."

"But they don't know how to find me. So I'm going to call them up and see if I can't help them with that."

THEY PARKED the CR-V behind Denison's garage and came in through the kitchen door. Denison and Bell were sitting at the island. Denison was wearing the same clothes he'd been wearing yesterday. He didn't look as if he'd slept very well. Bell wore a baby-blue robe with little cows printed on it. She was hunched over her coffee, gripping the cup as if it were her last hold on reality. She didn't look up. "Where were you two?" Denison asked.

"Tracking Nicole," Bryan said.

"Find her?" Denison asked.

"No such luck." Bryan and Cohen sat down at the island. Bryan filled them in.

"So there's gangsters after you, and that guy—Mr. White—pulled the chip from the phone," Denison said.

Bryan turned to Bell. "How do you feel today?"

"I still can't believe what happened. It's like a dream. Everything was in slow motion until Nicole yelled for me to run." Tears started down her cheeks.

Denison put his arm around her shoulders. "It's okay."

Bryan turned on the charm. "Yeah, slow motion, that's how it is sometimes." He nodded. "I'm sorry, Bell. I know you want to forget, to just blank the last two days out of your mind, but right now I have to ask you some questions so that we can help Nicole. Are you up for that?"

"I'll try my best."

"Great. This guy—Mr. White?"

She nodded.

"What can you tell me about him?"

"I don't know much. They kept me locked in a storeroom. It was like a basement."

"Anything could help."

She glanced at her father, and then looked at the floor. "The first night, he came into the storeroom thinking that I would have sex with him. Said it was no big deal, that he knew Nicole had sex for money. When I screamed, he tried to shut me up."

Denison's mouth fell open. "But the Doc said—"

"Nothing happened, Dad. The others came and made him leave."

"Really?" Denison asked.

She nodded. "None of them wanted him to hurt me." She covered her face with her hands. "And now they're dead."

"None of this was your fault," Denison said.

"I know, Dad. I know. I just can't get it out of my mind."

"Anything else?" Bryan asked.

"When they were leaving, I overheard the guy with the acne scars telling Fred Stein that Mr. White was crazy. I never saw him after that until you guys came to rescue me. When he had the gun on me and was pushing me up the stairs, I thought for sure I'd be raped and murdered."

"But you're safe now," Denison said.

Bell started crying. "With the other guys dead, there's no one to protect Nicole."

Denison held her and rubbed her back. Then he turned to Bryan. "When you go, I'm going with you."

"Absolutely not."

"I pushed her away, and it wasn't her fault."

"James, this isn't about you making yourself feel better. You're a civilian. You can't be part of this."

"How can you be so cool? He's got Nicole. I know she means everything to you."

"Yeah. You're right. She's my everything. I want to kill that asshole so bad that I can taste his blood in my mouth. But Nicole is still alive. I can feel it. And if I give in to my emotions, if I'm not thinking completely straight, I'm going to miss the chance to save her. And I'm not going to live with that." He took out his smartphone. "Let's see if he's put the chip back in her phone."

"Why would he do that?" Denison asked.

"Because he wants the money."

Bell started toward the hall. "I can't listen to any more of this. I'm going to my bedroom."

Bryan speed-dialed Nicole's phone. It rang and rang. Just as he thought it was about to go to voice mail, a man's voice said, "Yeah?"

"You ready to deal?"

"Guessed you were looking for me. I pulled the chip from this phone to make it a little more interesting."

"And now you put the chip back in, so you must want to talk. Arithmetic is working in your favor. You went from a four-way split to a no-way split."

"Lost my partners, though. And maybe I want to be spiteful, teach you a lesson."

"I thought this was business."

"There's some of that too. So you finally got the money?"

"Yeah."

"I'm going to be on safe ground this time."

"Bring Nicole, unharmed, we'll bring the hundred grand."

"Unharmed? It's a little late for that. I'll call back at midnight."

The phone went dead. Denison and Cohen were looking at him. "We're in business."

"How's Nicole?" Denison asked.

"Don't know. I'm not going to lie, James. I'm sure Nicole told you this. Crazy people act crazy. There's nothing we can do except play our hand the best way we can. Now for the other guys."

IN A RUNDOWN MOTEL ROOM, Nicole was naked, tied spread-eagle face down on the unmade bed, the sheets and bedspread in a tangle on the floor. Her mouth was gagged with a washcloth and duct tape, and her nose was swollen, making every breath difficult. All her tender places hurt. She was afraid and in pain and uncertain that she would escape with her life, but she was working her plan. Every time Mr. White came at her, she increased her advantage by acting more fearful, more broken, more beat down, as if he were more and more in control, but she was watching him, studying him, waiting for her chance. She didn't really believe her chance would ever come. She was more or less certain that she would die violated and battered. But her plan was all she had, so she couldn't give it up. And now, finally, Bryan was in the mix, shaping the details that would lead Mr. White to his death. At least she could count on that.

She watched Mr. White in the narrow line of light peeking through the curtains as he sat in his boxer shorts at the table by the window. He pulled the chip from her phone and set the phone and the chip down on the table. He looked over at her as if he were puzzling something out before he dragged his chair over to the bed. "That wasn't Denison. And it didn't sound like that big bastard." He poked her shoulder. "You didn't tell me about this guy, which pisses me off a little. He wants to trade you for the money. I'm going to take off your gag. If you yell, I'm going to hurt you."

He pulled the duct tape off her mouth. She spat out the washcloth.

"You're doing good. You keep on being good, and I'll give you a drink of water. Now then, who is this guy and how will he come at me?"

"He's my partner. He can be hard to figure."

"I bet. But you know all his moves."

"I do."

"So?"

She didn't reply.

"We've been over this. That big bastard killed my friends. You're lucky to be alive. You've got a lot of bruises. Do you want some fresh ones?"

She made her expression completely submissive. "He won't be choosing the ground, so he'll make the trade. If you don't blink, you'll leave with the money."

"But?"

"Tracker in the bag. After you think you're safe, he'll come to get the money back."

He ran his hand down her back. She trembled. "Let me get you that drink of water."

She watched him walk across the room to the bathroom. She'd done everything she could to misdirect him. He was as overconfident as possible. Now it was up to Bryan to spring his trap. She smiled to herself. Mr. White was a walking dead man.

BRYAN SAT on a stool at the kitchen island, the bottle of beer in front of him and his phone at his ear. Denison and Cohen sat watching him. "Connect me with room 179, please."

"Yeah?"

"You're chasing a grifter."

"Who the fuck are you?"

"We're trailing his partner. We'll sell him to you for ten grand."

"That is so much bullshit. You're just cops."

"Not the cops. Just looking to sell some good information."

"Why should we pay?"

"'Cause he's a pain in the ass that your boss wanted dead yesterday. You don't know where he is, do you? You've just got the car tag. But we're following his partner. You scoop him up, he tells you where to find the grifter, you kill him, and you all go back to doing your thing."

"Maybe."

"You better get on this train, brother. He leaves town; the trail will be ice cold again."

"We'll think about it."

"I'll call back with a time and place."

Bryan set his phone down on the granite counter and took a drink of beer.

"They actually buy it?" Cohen asked.

"He's thinking. I'm lucky about this sort of thing. Just wait and see."

Denison looked at him as if he were trying to understand a math problem that was just a little too complicated. "So your plan, if I understand correctly, is to use a gang of drug criminals who are hunting you to kill the psycho who has Nicole?"

"That's exactly what I plan to do—if I can pull it off."

"I understand how this helps you—some of the drug criminals might be killed—but how does it help Nicole?"

"This asshole is expecting us. He's expecting to have the advantage because we don't want him to kill Nicole. So the drug thugs with their demands—he won't have the slightest idea what they're talking about—will throw him off guard."

"But he might kill Nicole."

"James, he's going to kill Nicole. There's no doubt about that. His plan is to get the money, kill her, and kill us, if he can. Because otherwise that sick fuck knows I'm hunting him down. Our task is to save Nicole before he can kill her. So he can't have the money, but he has to believe he's going to get it."

"But what will you do if the drug criminals won't go for it?"

"Think of something else. In the meantime, get the money. We'll need it with us when we go to the meet."

THE GANGSTER STOOD by the window of room 179 looking out into the parking lot. His guys were sitting around this shithole motel drinking beer and playing cards, when they should have been at home earning. Hunting for the grifter was taking too much time, cutting into his income. And the junky who'd seen the grifter at the airport was completely worthless. Her description could've been any old white man. And there wasn't any future in killing white men around here. There were the customers. He took out his burner phone. "Spanish? I got a lead. Guy says he can finger your boy's partner."

"He's not a cop?"

"No."

"Then what's holding you up?"

"When we catch your boy, how messy do you want it? How big a message you want to send?"

"No civilians. But the grifter and his people? I want the world to know what happens if you fuck with me."

"You got it."

BELL WOKE UP IN A FOG, the sleeping pill she'd taken dragging her down. She stood in her bedroom looking out the window at the sand and ocean and sky. She needed to get dressed, but she just couldn't seem to think through what she should wear. She glanced at the face of her smartphone. Three o'clock. She'd slept through lunch. The last forty-eight hours were—she couldn't even think of words to express what she felt. Bobby would be back in his office by now. He'd left two messages on her voice mail. She deleted them without listening to them, and then speed-dialed his number.

"Hey, beautiful," he said. "I was beginning to wonder what happened to you. Things must be going pretty well for you to not have time to call me back."

She sat down on the edge of the bed. "Are you alone?"

"Yeah."

She told him about her abduction and rescue.

"Jesus Christ. Your dad should have called me."

"He didn't tell anyone."

"But you're okay?"

"Yeah." Her voice was flat.

"I mean, crazy trauma, but physically—"

"Yeah."

"And Nicole's partner is there?"

"Bryan got here late last night. He and Cohen, they're like wolves. He's concocting a scheme to get Nicole back, talking to the last kidnapper on the phone. I just couldn't listen anymore."

"So Nicole and the other guy—Cohen—killed three of those guys. Why didn't your dad just pay?"

"Nicole said they were going to kill us after they got the money."

"Do you think that's true?"

"I don't know. That doesn't matter now. Nicole saved me. Dad's not going to turn on her. Besides, Nicole is Bryan's partner. I get the impression that's more than just business. So he's calling the shots."

"So your dad is helping killers. Does Skip know about any of this?"

"No. Dad's not going to tell him anything until it's all over. He doesn't want him to interfere."

"But you're really okay?"

"I'm doing better. After they rescued me, I felt so guilty about feeling relieved. God knows what that crazy guy is doing to Nicole."

"I'm coming out there. I'm going to get on the first plane."

"I need you so bad. I want you here with me, but you should wait. The next twenty-four hours are going to be insane."

"I'm coming out."

"Just stay on the phone with me until it's all over. If you're on the plane, I won't be able to hear your voice if I need you."

"Okay. If that's what you want. But I'm flying out tomorrow."

"Just wait, honey. I'll keep you in the loop on everything."

"Switch over to Facetime. I have to see you."

"I'm a mess. I just got up from a nap. I've got bedhead."

"I have to see how banged up you are."

"Okay." They switched over to Facetime. She could see his spectacled face and most of his reddish-blond beard. "Satisfied?"

"Show me your arms."

She moved her phone down her arms. "See? No bruises. I'm okay."

"You're going to answer the phone when I call."

"I know."

"No matter what's happening."

"I will." She air kissed him. "I love you."

"I love you."

13

THE TRAVEL ACE

At midnight Bryan's phone rang. He opened his eyes. Moonlight angled into the den from the east windows. He sat up in the chair where he'd been dozing, rubbed his face, and tried to shake off the dream he'd been in—a dream where he was running down a tunnel and couldn't reach the end. "Yeah?"

"That woman of yours has got some spirit. There's a Travel Ace truck stop at the freeway interchange on the east side of town. We meet back by the highway sign. Two hours. I'm leaving her there, alive or dead. It's up to you. You want her alive you bring the money."

Cohen was standing next to him in the dark. "Is it a go?"

Bryan got to his feet. "I've got to see how many pieces are going to be on the board."

They walked into the kitchen and turned on the light. Cohen got two beers out of the refrigerator, opened them, and passed one to Bryan. Bryan took a long, slow pull. Then he looked down at the counter and rubbed his hands together. He had to get this just right. There was no room for error. Nicole was as much a part of him as his hand or his heart. He had to get her back. He dialed the Weekender Motel. "Room 179, please."

The telephone rang over and over. Finally a sleepy voice said, "You're a dead man."

"You like sleeping in that shitty bed? You're lucky you don't have bedbugs."

"You're going to suffer first."

He heard a voice in the background, but it wasn't loud enough for him to tell if it was male or female. "You want to go home? I know where the grifter's partner is going to be in two hours. All you have to do is scoop him up, have a chat, and you'll know where the grifter is."

"I'm not paying you ten thousand dollars."

"How about five thousand?"

"Huh-uh."

"How about I get to keep his car, his wallet, and his gun?"

"Why do you hate this guy so much?"

"Do I have to have a reason?"

The man laughed.

"The grifter screwed me over. I was going to kill him myself, but then I saw you guys were on it. Decided to get out of the way."

"In two hours?"

"That's right."

"You want him gone; you should tell me for free."

Bryan paused, counted silently to ten, and then said, "Really? I can't have anything?"

"You can keep your life."

"There's a Travel Ace truck stop at the freeway interchange over on the east side of town. He'll be back by the highway sign. He'll have a woman with him. He thinks he's collecting a ransom."

"Your woman?"

"Yes."

"She better stay out of the way."

Bryan turned to Cohen as he slipped his phone into his pocket. "Let's gear up."

THE TRAVEL ACE truck stop was quiet except for the idling of the dozen or so tractor-trailer rigs parked in the back lot by the highway sign, and the quiet bartering of the prostitutes and drug dealers. Bryan and Cohen, dark clothes and Kevlar vests, stood in the shadow between two rigs, watching the base of the highway sign, which was lit up by parking-lot lights. There was no one in sight.

"Got here first," Cohen said.

"Yeah."

"What's your thinking?"

"This is not the best situation for us."

"Too much open ground around that sign."

"We can't have them talking to one another too long, so if they don't start shooting, we're going to have to help them along," Bryan said.

"I'll leave that to you. Once you start, I'll open up."

"Nobody's getting out of here alive, except Nicole."

"Got you. I'm going to set up next to that shed over to the right. It's a little distant, but the cover is good." Cohen pointed at a sheet-metal building with an outdoor light above the door. A row of evergreen bushes ran along the left side.

"I'm going to stay on the move."

Cohen nodded.

"And Cohen," Bryan said, "if the gangbangers don't kill him, he's mine."

Cohen smiled. "As long as he doesn't get in my way."

AT 1:00 A.M. the jeep drove into the halo of strong light at the base of the Travel Ace sign. Bryan could see two people in the gloom of the front seat, but he couldn't tell who they were. He glanced around. Most of the prostitutes and drug slingers were gone. The only noise was the idling of the diesel engines. He looked over at the sheet-metal shed. He couldn't see Cohen in the bushes, but he knew he was over there, waiting.

At 2:00 a.m. the yellow Lincoln came rolling across the parking lot. Bryan snuck among the parked semitrucks until he was crouching behind a wheel of the closest truck. Mr. White, wearing Nicole's Kevlar and carrying her MP5K submachine gun, pushed open the door to the Jeep and shoved Nicole out in front of him. She fell to the pavement. He pulled her to her feet and kept behind her. Her wrists and her knees were duct-taped. She was too far away for Bryan to see anything else. But she was alive, and that was all that mattered.

Four Latinos in work clothes climbed out of the Lincoln. Mr. White gripped Nicole around her waist with his free arm and pressed the submachine gun into her side. One of the men from the Lincoln shouted and gestured at Mr. White. He shouted something back.

The scene shifted into slow motion. A man wearing a black ball cap pulled a pistol from under his shirt. As he raised it up, Mr. White swung the submachine gun around and fired. Ball cap went down, his pistol firing wild. Nicole kicked free, rolled across the asphalt, and started crawling away. The other three men pulled pistols from their clothes and opened up on Mr. White, running forward as they fired. Bryan rolled under the truck to improve his position and started shooting. Another gangster went down.

Bryan heard firing from the right. Cohen was in the open, running at a crouch, firing the MP5K in bursts. Another gangster fell, then Mr. White, then the final gangster. Bryan scrambled out from under the truck and ran to Nicole. Cohen moved cautiously, scanning the fallen men for movement. When he got to Mr. White, he prodded him with his boot. Mr. White's head rocked back and forth. Cohen whistled to Bryan and then pointed down at Mr. White. Bryan gave a quick wave. He turned back to Nicole, who was still crawling away, flopping along like fish on dry land.

"Hey," Bryan said. He flipped her onto her back. "I've got you."

She was panting, out of breath, but still struggling. "Hey, it's me. I've got you," he said.

Her expression shifted. "Bryan."

"I'm right here. I'm cutting you free. Just give me a second." He put his Glock into her hands, pulled his lock-back knife, and cut through the duct tape. She sat up.

"Take it easy," he said. He put his arms around her and held her. "Sorry I took so long. You look pretty banged up."

"I'm not talking about it."

Bryan studied her face. Her cheek was bruised, and her lip was bloody, but the emptiness in her eyes told him what she'd been through. "That bad?"

"Yeah."

"Can you walk?"

She winced as she got to her feet. Bryan took her by the elbow. "Lean on me," he said.

She pulled away. "I don't need any help."

Cohen stood over Mr. White, pointing the submachine gun as his face. "He's bleeding pretty good."

Mr. White had a neck wound and multiple wounds to his legs.

Bryan glanced around. Lights were coming on in the cabs of nearby trucks. "We can't hang around. We can leave the bangers and the Lincoln. But this one is the odd man out. Help me put him in the Jeep. Then you follow me in the Honda."

Cohen and Bryan picked Mr. White up by his arms and legs and shoved him into the backseat of the Jeep. Nicole climbed in the passenger's side. Bryan drove away from the truck stop. The night seemed suddenly quiet and peaceful. No more gunfire. No police sirens. He couldn't believe they'd actually gotten away with it. Crap odds from the get-go. And yet here they were. He got on the freeway heading north and took the third off-ramp, which led onto a county road. He glanced at Nicole, who was leaning up against the door. She stank of fear and sex.

"I'm so glad to have you back."

"I knew you'd come, but I didn't know. Know what I mean?"

"It was touch-and-go for a minute there. How bad you hurt?"

"I'm okay."

"I'd say your boy is one sick puppy."

She sniffled and turned away.

"What you going to tell Denison?"

"I don't know."

"You should have let Mr. White take her."

"It was my choice."

"I know. You couldn't tell Denison that you'd lost his daughter. You got in too deep. Started caring about them. That's why you couldn't wait for me."

"It's worse than that. I think maybe I love him."

"Then it's a good thing he's your retirement plan."

Bryan pulled off the road and drove down to the edge of a pasture. He turned off the Jeep. Cohen was walking toward them with a five-gallon gas can. "Time to shoot this bastard."

"I can't do it."

"Yes, you can."

"No, I can't."

"I can't do it for you."

She shook her head. "I'm not ready."

"Honey, I know it's hard. But it's yours to do."

She got up on her knees to look into the backseat. Mr. White was still unconscious. His neck and the seat were sticky with blood. She thought about how he'd beaten her unconscious, tied her down, raped her until she woke up and struggled, and then beat her some more. He'd almost broken her. He probably would have if he had more time. She took a deep breath and shot him twice in the face. Then she sat back down and handed the Glock to Bryan.

"Good for you," he said. "Let's get out of here."

Cohen poured the gas over the interior of the Jeep and threw the gas can inside when it was empty. Bryan lit a piece of paper with a lighter and tossed it in. They stood on the shoulder of the road watching the fire eat through the interior before they got in the Honda and drove back into town. A line of red colored the horizon. Bryan looked over his shoulder into the backseat. Nicole was sitting in the corner with her arms around her knees, looking small and vulnerable.

DENISON WAS PEERING through a gap in the curtains when the Honda pulled down the driveway and into the backyard. Bell was in bed. The doctor, her black hair pulled back in a loose ponytail, was sitting at the kitchen island drinking coffee, her medical kit on the island next to her. Nicole stumbled in the back door, one arm wrapped around her ribs. Bryan and Cohen were right behind her.

"Nicki," Denison said, "I'm so happy to see you." He moved toward her to hug her.

Nicole held up her other hand to hold him off. "Not now."

He saw her bruised face and the pain in her eyes. "Christ, you need a doctor."

"I'm fine."

"You're in shock."

She leaned against the kitchen island. The doctor gave her an appraising look. "I'm Dr. Kelly. I'm here to help you."

She studied the doctor for a moment. "Okay. Let's go to my room."

They disappeared down the hall.

Denison turned to Bryan. "What happened to her?"

"She was in a shit storm. She's banged up and exhausted."

"There's more to it than that."

Bryan got two beers out of the refrigerator, opened them, and passed one to Cohen. They clinked bottles before they drank. Bryan turned to Denison. "We need a couple of black garbage bags."

"You've got to tell me more," Denison said.

"I don't know much," Bryan said, "and it would be better if Nicole told you. In the meantime, we need large garbage bags."

Denison disappeared into the mudroom. Bryan pulled off his Kevlar vest, kicked off his boots, took another drink, and unzipped his pants. Denison came back with the bags. Bryan stripped down to his underwear, and then put his clothing into one of the bags. Cohen followed suit. "Weapons too?"

Bryan nodded. He unloaded the Glock and the submachine gun, wiped them down, and put them back in their cases. Bryan walked down the hallway in his underwear and knocked on Nicole's door. The doctor peeked out.

"I need her clothes," Bryan said.

The doctor closed the door and came back in a minute with Nicole's clothes. Bryan carried them back down the hall. In the kitchen, the TV was turned to the local news. The lead stories were the murders at the beach house and the gunfight at the truck stop. They hadn't found out about the Jeep fire yet.

IN NICOLE'S BEDROOM, Nicole sat on the edge of the king-size bed in her panties, her hair sticking out in odd directions. Red-blue bruises shaped like fingers circled her throat and her side bore a hand-size bruise where her ribs had been cracked by the gunshot. Her thighs were scratched, and her panties were stained. The doctor was standing in front of her. "Ms. Carter, I don't have a rape kit with me. All these wounds should be documented. You should go to the emergency room and file a police report."

"I'm not going to the hospital."

The doctor sighed. "You're on the pill?"

"Yes."

"The pain meds should help. I've given you the standard STI meds, but without testing there's no way to know if we've covered everything." The doctor shook her head. "You need to go to the hospital."

"I'll be fine. You can go now. I'm going to shower and change."

"I'm not going to leave you alone."

Nicole shrugged. She went into the bathroom. She felt as if she were walking on the bottom of a swimming pool, the air buffeting her like currents of water, the sounds muffled and distant. She could still feel Mr. White's penis in her anus and in her vagina, still felt physically raw, as if he were still raping her right now. She knew that feeling would go away. But the feeling of being controlled, owned, helpless in the most intimate way—that feeling of wanting to curl up in the corner of the shower sobbing with the water raining down and wanting to stay there forever—that was the feeling she had to hide. Right now she felt as if coming here at all —involving herself with Denison and his family—had been a mistake, even though she knew those feelings were not true. She took a deep breath and felt a stab of pain from her cracked ribs. She felt the gun in her hand as she squeezed the trigger. Reality shifted.

She combed out her wet hair and put on a pair of pajama pants and a long-sleeve top. There was no point in trying to hide the neck bruises. The doctor walked beside her as she shuffled into the kitchen. Bryan and Cohen were in their street clothes. A black garbage bag and the gun cases were stacked at the door to the mudroom. Cohen sat at the end of the island nursing a beer, watching her, catlike. Bryan stood in the middle of the island with a glass of whiskey in his hand.

Denison gasped. He stepped toward her, his eyes afraid, his mouth half-open like he wanted to say something but didn't know what to say. She avoided his hug, but let him take her arm and guide her to a stool.

"Your throat," he said.

Bryan glanced at Cohen. "I told you she was a fighter." He poured whiskey into a glass and pushed it toward her.

The doctor got an ice pack from the freezer and handed it to Nicole. "Ice the cracked ribs twenty minutes for every hour you're awake today and then three times a day for the next week. And alcohol is a bad idea."

Nicole put the ice pack up against her ribs, but she couldn't feel the cold.

The doctor turned to Denison. "She belongs in a hospital, but she refused. Keep an eye on her. If you need anything else, give me a call."

"Thank you," Denison said.

Nicole picked up the glass of whiskey with her free hand and drank it down. The heat exploded in her belly. Bryan poured her another one. She held it in her hand, using it as a prop, deciding only at that moment that she was going to play it straight with Denison, maybe not tell him everything, not yet anyway, but not lie.

"So," Denison asked, "are you going to tell me what happened?"

"I was in the kitchen when Mr. White was leaving with Bell. We scuffled. He was a big boy. He got a hand free and shot me in the vest. The doc says two cracked ribs."

Denison smiled grimly.

"He was angry. We'd killed his friends. I wouldn't cooperate. He put a beating on me."

"And that's all?"

She sipped her whiskey.

"Nicki, you're not protecting me by not talking." He reached for her hand. She pulled away. His face turned red, and his eyes teared up. "He raped you."

She looked down at the swirls in the granite counter. "I can't talk about it right now."

"But I want to help." Denison reached for Nicole's hand again, and this time she let him take it. "If you hadn't pulled her out of the way, it would have been Bell."

"Jimmy, if our relationship is going to be about you feeling grateful, I can't deal with that."

"But what you did—I just lost Stacey. Now I almost lost you."

"You've got to let it go." She drank down her whiskey. Bryan poured her another one. "I need some breakfast."

Denison thumbed the tears out of the corners of his eyes. "I can't understand you people."

"Have a drink," Bryan said.

Denison shook his head.

"Then make yourself useful. What kind of breakfast stuff do you have here?"

LATER THAT MORNING, Bryan and Cohen sat in the Honda at the airport departures entrance. Cars were pulling up to unload travelers. Families were hugging goodbye on the sidewalk. The voice on the PA system was advising people not to park in front of the terminal. Cohen had his hand on the door handle. "It was a pleasure doing business with you."

"Same here."

"Shame about your partner."

"She's tougher than she looks."

"I know she can handle herself, but that's not what I meant."

Bryan shrugged. "It's probably going to take a while."

"You need my services, you've got my good email."

"Twenty K for a couple of days work."

Cohen smiled. "Works for me."

"Good luck."

Cohen slammed the car door shut. Bryan watched him walk into departures, his carry-on over his shoulder, before he pulled away from the curb. He hadn't seen anyone suspicious out in front of the airport, didn't believe he'd picked up a tail, but he drove the Honda back into long-term parking and stole a new car, a Subaru Outback, just to be on the safe side.

MIDAFTERNOON, Bryan, Nicole, Denison, and Bell sat around the kitchen island, the remnants of lunch scattered before them. Nicole was still in her pajamas. A half-eaten turkey sandwich sat on her plate next to most of a serving of cantaloupe. Her bruises looked better, but she was jittery, unable to settle, wary of sudden movements or sounds. Bryan topped off her glass of white wine. Denison watched her while trying to act like he wasn't watching her, his face washed out and sad. They all seemed strangely unaffected by their drinking, except for Bell, who couldn't stop babbling.

"So Fred Stein told me things about you that I don't want to believe."

"Like what?" Nicole asked.

"That you pretended to be his girlfriend."

"It's true."

"So you slept with him?"

"Yes."

"For no other reason than to cheat him?"

"Yes."

"How do you do that?"

"Bell," Denison said, "that's enough."

"It's okay, James," Nicole said. "It's a lot to process."

"He said you were always on the scam. That's why Mr. White—that's why Mr. White thought I'd have sex with him."

Bell got off her stool, picked up her plate as if she were going to take it to the dishwasher, then set it back down, and enveloped Nicole in a gigantic hug. "I love you," she said.

Nicole winced. She put up her arms to push Bell away. "You're drunk. Please let go of me."

Bell loosened her hug and kissed Nicole's cheek. "You saved me. I thought you wanted to hurt my dad, but you shoved me out of the way, told me to run." She started to sob.

Nicole gently pushed her away.

Denison came around the island and took Bell in his arms. "It's okay, honey. It's okay."

Bryan watched Nicole watching them. He put his hand on her shoulder. "It's tough watching her give in to her vulnerability, isn't it? To us, it's a weakness to be exploited, but sometimes, if you want to get yourself back, it's what you've got to do."

"I can't do it. I could act it, if you like, but I can't do it." She drank off her wine.

THAT EVENING Nicole stood at the railing of the deck by the swimming pool watching the waves roll up the beach. She'd managed to slip away after supper, and no one had followed her. It was a relief to finally be alone. Right now, in this moment, she didn't have to pretend she felt better than she really did. Her tender places still hurt when she moved. She'd been drinking all day, but it hadn't drowned out the immediacy of the physical and emotional nightmare that still haunted her. Mr. White was at the edge of her peripheral vision, taunting her, doing everything he could think of to break her. Even though the night was warm and humid, goose bumps broke out on her arms.

She heard the door open. Denison came out on the deck carrying two martini glasses.

"Thought you might want a martini."

"Thanks." She held the glass in both hands.

"You've been quiet all evening. How are you doing?"

"Really? Dragging myself out of the abyss."

"How's that working out?"

"It's harder than I want it to be."

"If you want to talk to a professional, I can have someone here tomorrow."

"I appreciate that, James."

"I'd do anything for you. You just tell me, and I'll make it happen."

She set her glass down on the railing, looked out at the churning ocean, and offered Denison her hand. He took it. She felt the warmth and solidity of it, the softness of his palm and the hardness of the row of callous on his fingers. "You're a wonderful man, Jimmy."

He stammered. "How? I don't—I'm the one who's supposed to be comforting you."

"And you are. You don't have to say anything. Just stand here and breathe and hold my hand."

NICOLE WOKE up in the dark. She could hear a muffled thump, then a metallic click, and a sound like a window being raised. She rolled off the bed and padded to the door, but she couldn't find the doorknob. She felt along the wall, trying to find the edge of the door so that she could slide her hand down to the knob, but the door just wasn't there. Finally she realized that she'd gotten turned around somehow—that the door was on the other side of the room. Now she was out in the hall. She could feel a breeze coming from the living room. Where was everyone?

She crept down the hall and slipped into the living room. Only it wasn't the living room anymore. It was the dressing room of a clothing shop. Dresses on hangars hung along the walls. Pants and tops were stacked on the chairs. Underwear was piled in the floor. How long had she been here?

She'd been trying to get dressed for the longest time, but she couldn't seem to find the underwear that went with the outerwear so that she could leave the dressing room. She banged on the door, called for the clerk, but it made no difference.

She was running down a cobblestone alley. A ghost was chasing her. Trashcans stood by the padlocked doors and debris was piled against the walls. Up ahead, at the cross-street, was her car. She could see Bryan behind the wheel. She was running, running as fast as she could, but her clothes were too tight—they weren't meant for running—and the ghost was gaining on her. Who was the ghost? Why was he chasing her? Why was the car so far away? Her foot caught on something. She stumbled, lost her balance, rolled across the cobblestones. Her knees and the palm of her hands were bloody. She spat blood. She looked up. There was something in her hand.

SHE WAS STANDING in the dark in Denison's bedroom, holding a carving knife. Denison lay in bed, snoring softly. Was she dreaming? She felt a hand on her shoulder, gasped, and pivoted on her left foot as she raised the knife to strike.

"Whoa," Bryan whispered. "I saw you moving down the hall."

He led her out of Denison's room and down the hall to the kitchen, where the nightlight in the range hood was on. Nicole was naked, the scars and bruises on her body ghoulish in the dim light.

Bryan smiled. "It's been a long time since you sleepwalked. You remember anything?"

"Being chased."

Bryan padded over to the sink, filled a glass with water, and brought it to her. She drained the glass and set it on the counter.

"I believe that knife goes there," Bryan said, nodding at the knife block on the counter.

"How long were you watching me?"

"Ten minutes, maybe. Heard noise in the hall. At first I thought you were headed for the comfort of Denison's bed, but then you started moving around like you thought you were somewhere else."

She leaned her elbows on the kitchen island, resting her face in her hands. "God, I'm a mess. I haven't had a dream like that in years."

"Do you want to get into Denison's bed?"

"I don't think I could stand to have another person touch me, even accidentally. And now I'm a little bit afraid to go to sleep."

"You wouldn't have hurt him."

"You know that?"

"Yeah."

"It's worse this time."

"Maybe. Always seems worse until it's over. Put your robe on. There's still another bottle of whiskey around here. We'll sit in the den and watch the night until you're ready to lay down."

She put her hand on his shoulder and tried to see into his eyes. "Do you really think I'm going to be okay?"

"Yes. You're going to be okay. Because we're going to do whatever it takes to get you there. Right? It's me and you. Always us."

He got the bottle of whiskey and two glasses and sat down on the sofa in the den. She came back wrapped in an oversize terrycloth robe. They watched the stars and the distant lights of the boats on the water and listened to the surf pound the beach. Neither said a word. In the early dim before true morning, just as they began to see the seagulls moving, she lay her head in his lap and closed her eyes. He stroked her hair and sipped his drink. As she drifted off she found herself back in the motel room, tied down on the bed, Mr. White's hands around her throat as he raped her from behind. She started whimpering. Bryan lay his hand on her shoulder. She opened her eyes, shuddered and began to sob. Then she hugged his thigh with both her arms and bawled. He rubbed her back.

Denison appeared in the doorway in his pajamas, still half-asleep, alarm spreading over his face.

"It's okay," Bryan said. "Nothing to worry about."

WHEN NICOLE GOT UP, it was already afternoon. Everyone was gathered around the kitchen island: Denison, Bryan, Bell, and her boyfriend, Bobby, a red-bearded bear of a man with gold, wire-rimmed glasses. They were all drinking champagne.

"There you are," Denison said. "We were just toasting Bell's engagement."

"Well, congratulations," Nicole said.

Bell poured champagne into a flute and Bell and Bobby scooted over so that Nicole could sit next to Denison.

"This is my boyfriend, Bobby. Or I guess I should say my fiancé."

"Pleased to meet you." Nicole tried to smile, but she felt a claustrophobic desperation settling around her. She wasn't sure she could be around so many people. She put her hand on top of Bryan's. "Is there any whiskey left?"

Bryan poured whiskey and passed it to her. She took a long drink. Everyone was watching her.

"Feeling any better?" Denison asked.

"Than yesterday? Yes. Sorry about this morning. I just—it just came out."

Bell squeezed her hand. "You've got nothing to feel sorry about."

Nicole could see Mr. White in her peripheral vision. She drank some more whiskey to push him away.

"Would you like an omelet?" Denison asked.

Nicole took a deep breath. The whiskey was doing its work. She began to feel more relaxed. "Yes. Please."

"What do you want in it?" Denison asked. "There's cheese, olives, green peppers, ham."

"Everything. And a glass of milk."

LATER, after dinner, Nicole wandered into Bryan's room, a glass of whiskey in her hand. All day long, her ordeal had been flashing back in her mind, bowling her over emotionally, and she'd been struggling to contain the emotions, to take control of those nightmarish memories and pack them into a tiny bundle that she could push into a far corner of her mind until she felt strong enough to deal with them. The memories were still flashing out at her when she least expected, but she was feeling stronger and knew now what she had to do. She needed Bryan—needed the certainty that he provided that she had value, could create value. She needed him because he needed her, always needed her, and his need proved that her feelings of worthlessness were a lie.

Bryan looked up from folding a shirt into his open suitcase. "Still hard drinking?"

"'Til tomorrow. You leaving?"

"Yeah. First thing in the morning. Now that this business is settled, I'm going back for the safe-deposit-box money and some payback."

"I'm going with you."

He stopped what he was doing. "Have you thought this through? You don't get over what you've been through in just a day or two. The daughter's your best girlfriend now. The son doesn't stand a chance. This was supposed to be my gift to you. Your retirement package."

"You going corporate?"

"I can't promise you another deal like this."

"I'm not giving this up."

"Good."

"You just can't admit that you need my help."

"Oh, I need you. I was unarmed, up to my chest in a creek, with guys coming to kill me needing you. Do you think those bastards would have been able to dog me if you were with me? Neither of us is one hundred percent without the other."

Her eyes lit up. "Then it's settled." She put her whiskey on the night table, hugged him tight, closed her eyes, and breathed in his scent.

He stroked her hair. "I just want what's best for you."

She kissed him with her eyes open. "Tomorrow, then."

She drifted down the hall past the kitchen and into the den, drinking as she went. Bell, Bobby, and Denison were on the sofa watching a news channel, Bell nestled against Bobby as if she were a little girl. She shifted over when she saw Nicole and patted the cushion between her and her father. "Come, sit."

Nicole plopped down between them. Denison turned off the TV. "How you doing?"

"I'm okay. As long as I don't feel too much I can keep moving forward."

"I know you need your space right now, but if you need anything or want to talk about anything..."

"Jimmy, don't worry. I know you're here for me. I just can't talk about it right now. It hurts too much."

No one spoke for a few minutes. Finally, Bell said, "So Bryan's leaving in the morning?"

"Yeah," Nicole replied.

"What do you want to do tomorrow?" Denison asked. "Bell and Bobby will be here a few more days."

"That's what I need to talk to you about. I'm going with Bryan," Nicole said.

"Nicki, I want you to stay. What do I need to do to get you to stay?" Denison asked.

"You need to stay at least until you get well," Bell said.

"I can't. I need to go with Bryan. It's the only way I'm going to heal."

"I remember," Denison said. "You and Bryan. We've talked about this. He's your center. He makes you stronger."

"Sitting out by the pool. That seems like such a long time ago."

"That's why you could cry." Denison's face crumpled. "But what about us?"

She tried to smile her old bright smile. "You haven't gotten rid of me. I've got your cell number, so if you're not here, I'll be able to find you."

"Can I call you?" Denison asked.

"Jimmy, of course you can call me." She forced herself to kiss him. "You can always call me. You're my guy."

"Sit with us awhile."

She shook her head. "I'm going to my room."

"I love you," he said.

"I love you too."

Bobby watched Nicole shuffle away. He turned to Bell and her father. "She's a wreck. The woman you described over the phone and that woman—hard to believe they're the same person."

Bell nodded. "She looks ten years older than she did when I came here."

"When you told me what happened to you—that you'd been kidnapped, that your dad was working with criminals instead of calling the police—I thought about how crazy dangerous the whole thing was and how lucky you were to be safe. I thought I understood what was at stake, what the worst could be, but I was wrong. I didn't know at all. And now I can't even express how grateful I am that what happened to her didn't happen to you."

Bell hugged him.

Denison's eyes were wet. "You can't even say the words, can you? It's so bad you've got to talk in circles around it."

"Raped," Bobby said.

Bell shook her head. "That doesn't begin to describe what happened to her. That's just something that was done to her. It's like she's not in color anymore. She's the black-and-white version of herself."

"God," Denison said, "if she hadn't chosen to push you out of the way. I want to help her so much. And now it looks like I'm going to lose her."

"No, Dad. She really loves you. She'll be back."

"I can't compete with Bryan."

"You don't have to compete with Bryan. For her, you're not the same."

14

TIDYING UP

Bryan and Nicole flew into Indianapolis, rented a car, and took their time working their way back to Springville, switching cars twice before buying a black Cadillac. One evening, they stopped at a chain motel at a freeway interchange and went into the Play Ball! sports bar for supper. It appeared to be the local watering hole. The bar was crowded with a diverse group: suits, dress casual, and work clothes. Their server, a young woman in a black-and-white striped referee's shirt, with her bleached-blonde hair pinned up on the top of her head, led them to a booth on the far wall.

"Something to drink other than water?" she asked.

"Gin martini, two olives, no rocks," Nicole said.

"Me too," Bryan said.

She left them with their menus. They sat for a few minutes without speaking while they slowly scanned the room. There was no one there for them to be afraid of.

"How are you feeling?" Bryan asked.

"Honestly? My throat feels a little tight. There's too many people in here. I'll feel better after I drink my martini."

"You're of no use to either of us right now."

"I know."

"You've got to get back into the game. If you're not ready, you can always go back to Denison. He'll take care of you. But if you want to stay with me, you've got to be able to play your part."

"What have you got in mind?"

"See the cowboy at the bar?"

She glanced at the crowded bar. A big man with a grey mustache wearing a tan cowboy hat and highly polished cowboy boots sat at a stool about a quarter of the way down.

"Think you can take his watch?"

"I'm not in the mood."

"Not in the mood or not up to the challenge? You've got nothing to fear. We're both armed. This is just a nice little test run."

"Doesn't have to be that particular guy, does it? Let me drink my drink and eat something first."

Their server brought their martinis. "Ready to order?"

"I'll have the chicken burrito," Nicole said.

"The bacon cheeseburger for me," Bryan said. "And let me sub a side salad for the fries."

They clicked glasses and sipped their martinis. Nicole sighed. "So you want me to do a grab and drop?"

Bryan shrugged. "It's not a wrist lift, but it's a start. Breathe in, breathe out. You can do this. It's just like falling off a log."

Nicole looked at the bar. There was a full-figured, middle-aged woman with a beauty salon hairdo sitting next to the cowboy. Her handbag was hanging off the back of her stool. Easy pickings. But Nicole heard Mr. White's voice in her head. He was telling her she was worthless—second-rate, a whore, not a grifter. How else could he have caught her? She felt the hypervigilance creeping in. *She saw the woman turning toward her just as she was reaching into the woman's handbag, heard her yell, saw herself shifting to avoid being grabbed, rushing toward the door, being tackled by a bartender before she could push out into the parking lot.*

She gulped her martini. "Here goes."

Nicole's heart was racing as she moved toward the full-figured woman at the bar. She bumped into her, apologized profusely, and walked away with her car keys, which she flashed at Bryan. She went into the ladies' room and sat on the toilet. Her hands were shaking. She'd learned how to lift keys a long time ago, when she was just a kid. Bryan had showed her how. She thought she could do it in her sleep. But today, with Mr. White's voice in her ear, she wasn't sure of anything. She put her hand on her heart and took a slow, deep breath. She'd done the grab, now it was time for the drop. This had always been the easy part. She came out of the restroom, noted the gap between the middle-aged woman and the next bar stool, and crowded up into it. She held a hand up for the bartender. He had an expectant look on his face.

"You sell cigarettes?"

He shook his head. "Machine over by the door."

She turned to look, jostling the woman's handbag, and dropped the car keys back in. Then she returned to Bryan at the booth. "Satisfied?"

"Always a pleasure to watch you work. How did it feel?"

"A little rocky."

He saw that her hand was trembling and put his hand on hers. "He can't hurt you anymore."

"I know."

"You killed him."

"He's still crowding into my mind."

"But you felt that good rush, didn't you? When you dropped the keys and walked away?"

"Yeah, I did. It felt good."

"We're going to get you back on track. This isn't about what you can do; it's about pushing him out. You'll see. He doesn't know you. He doesn't know what you're capable of. We'll pull a few more practice runs along the way, and you'll be just fine."

A WEEK AND A HALF LATER, they sat in the Cadillac on the street half a block down from Neal Robertson's law offices. They'd been surveilling the offices for three days. Bryan was still clean-shaven.

Nicole wore a shoulder-length blonde wig. A white silk scarf wound around her throat hid what remained of the neck bruises. The day was already hot. They watched as the secretary and the new assistant left for lunch.

"You ready for this?" Bryan asked.

"Already getting a good feeling."

"You could wait in the car."

"No way. I need this."

"Then let's do it."

They put on throwaway latex gloves, got out of the car, and crossed the street, two black suits with pistols holstered under their jackets. Robertson was in his office working at his desk when they walked in.

"I'm sorry," he said, "we're closed over the lunch hour. I'm just about to leave. Call later to make an appointment."

They kept moving toward him. "We know you're closed," Bryan said. "That's why we're here."

Robertson jerked open his top desk drawer. "Who are you?"

Nicole pulled her Glock. "We've come for the safe-deposit-box key."

Bryan came around the desk and took the Colt .357 from the desk drawer.

"Are you crazy?" Robertson said. "You take that key, you'll be dead before nightfall."

"We'll take our chances," Bryan said.

"Don't you know that I'm protected?"

"Molly was a friend of mine."

Robertson's jaw dropped open. "You're the guy they've been looking for. Hey, I'm sorry about Molly. Sorry as I can be."

"I saw her shot and dumped in a hole up in Coon River State Park. Fighting to keep from being raped. So, yeah, I know how sorry you are."

"I didn't do that. I accidentally shot the boyfriend during the shakedown—"

"I'm not interested in your excuses. I want the key."

"It's in the safe."

"Where's the safe?"

"Over there, behind those books." He pointed to the bookshelves next to the sofa.

"Open it."

"Don't shoot me."

Robertson pulled down a row of law books, revealing a small wall safe. While he input the combination, Bryan stood behind him with his Glock pointed into Robertson's neck, and Nicole stood back to one side with her Glock pointed at the mass of Robertson's body.

"There's no gun in here," Robertson said.

"There better not be," Bryan replied.

Robertson opened the safe. Bryan pushed him toward Nicole. He took out some files, which he tossed on the carpet, an envelope of cash, which he put in his jacket pocket without counting, and a key to a bank safe-deposit box.

"Is this the key?"

"Yes."

He gave Robertson a push. He stepped back. "Which bank?"

"Milton."

He gave him another little push. "Molly still on the safe-deposit-box list?"

"Yeah." He looked from Bryan to Nicole and back again. "But how's that going to help?"

Bryan glanced at Nicole. "You believe him?"

She nodded. "Yes. Yes, I do."

"Sit back down."

Robertson sat down behind his desk.

"You know," Bryan said, "You are one careless motherfucker. I wonder what Spanish Mike would say if he knew that list wasn't updated? When I first started thinking about making this visit, I was going to leave you tied in that chair. Let you get a taste of what you did to Molly—a ride in a car trunk, a shaky walk to a shallow grave, three or four guys standing around laughing at you like you're there for their personal amusement."

"Please," Robertson said. "Please. I can get you money. Lots of money."

"But before you went on that ride, Spanish Mike would have an excellent description of us. The first little slap, and you'd be begging to tell what you know. The gratification is just not worth the risk. Molly would understand." He glanced at Nicole. "What time is it?"

"Twelve-thirty."

He shot Robertson twice in the chest and once in the face. "Time to go."

They strolled out the office door and across the street to the Cadillac. A few clouds were drifting across the sky. "It's so much fun working with you," Bryan said. "I just feel so much more confident knowing that you've got my back."

Nicole smiled and took his hand. "Whether I'm with you or not, I'm always going to have your back."

"Let's do some banking."

On the drive over to Milton Bank, they stopped at a Pick-N-Pay. Nicole went into the ladies' room with a canvas tote bag and locked the door. She took off the blonde wig and her black suit, folded them into the bag, and put on some padding to fill out her hips and her bust. Then she put on a teal dress and black sweater suitable to an office assistant, and styled her hair to match Molly's. A few touch-ups to her makeup, and she could pass for Molly if anyone at the bank happened to remember the one time she had been there.

Bryan pulled up to the front as she came out of the building. "You're a magician."

"Don't jinx it."

"I'm not jinxing it. I'm just telling the truth."

It was 1:30 p.m. when they pulled into a parking space away from the security camera at Milton Bank. There were three cars in the parking lot, all parked away from the doors. "You set?" Bryan asked.

"I'm ready to go."

"Knock 'em dead."

The bank was empty. Nicole walked up to the teller counter carrying a canvas tote. She felt hyperaware, almost as if she was outside her body watching herself work. Mr. White was nowhere to be found. She took a slow breath and fell into her role. The teller, a young woman wearing designer glasses, smiled at her. "Welcome to Milton Bank. How can I help you?"

"I'm Molly Wright. I'm from Mr. Robertson's office. I need access to the safe-deposit box."

"Do you have a key?"

She held up the key. "Yes."

"Are you on the list?"

She nodded.

The teller came out from behind the counter. "Follow me."

Nicole followed her into a vault lined with safe-deposit boxes of various sizes. The teller took out the list of people allowed to access Robertson's safe-deposit box, saw the name *Molly Wright* and asked Nicole for a picture ID. Nicole produced a forged ID. The teller had her sign and date the box access list. Nicole forged Molly's signature.

"Do you need a viewing room?"

"Yes."

The teller used Nicole's key and the bank's key to open the safety deposit box, slid out the drawer, and carried it into a room the size of a closet that contained a built-in counter and a stool. She set the drawer on the counter. "Let me know when you're ready to leave."

Nicole locked the door and lifted the lid on the box. It was full of fat envelopes. She opened the top one. Inside was a half-inch thick, banded bundle of one-hundred-dollar bills—$10,000. She counted the envelopes out onto the counter. Thirty-two, which meant $320,000. She opened her tote. She only had $200,000 in banded bundles of counterfeit hundreds. She swapped the counterfeit for the genuine, emptying and filling the envelopes, put the counterfeit into the drawer first, and then covered it with the $120,000 she couldn't swap. She stepped back out into the hall, where the teller was waiting for her. "All done?"

Nicole handed her the drawer. The teller took the drawer back into the security-deposit-box vault and brought Nicole's key back to her. "Anything else I can help you with?"

"No, thanks. That's all."

Nicole strolled out of the bank and climbed back into the Cadillac. She felt giddy. This was the way every job should go.

"All good?" Bryan asked.

"All good."

He backed out of the parking spot.

"There was three-hundred-twenty thousand in the box."

He pulled out into traffic. "So we left a hundred-twenty thousand."

"Yeah. I put the good stuff on top."

He chuckled. "Two hundred K."

"Do you want to pick up some more counterfeit and go back for the rest?"

"Let's not get greedy. When Robertson's found dead, everything is going to go crazy. It's time to leave town."

TWO WEEKS LATER, Bryan and Nicole stood in the shower together in a one-bedroom timeshare at Vista Lake Villages. No one was after them. Neal Robertson had vanished from the face of the earth, which meant the somehow Spanish Mike had gotten there ahead of the police. And according to the news reports, all the bodies at Cricket Bay had been conveniently filed under gang warfare. They stood under the spray together, saying nothing, just holding hands, their eyes closed. Finally, Nicole turned off the shower. Bryan looked her over, slowly turning her in a circle. "All healed. One new scar, but not a big one."

She kissed him lightly. "It's time for me to get back to James."

"I know."

She gave him a quizzical look.

"You've got your spirit back."

"Mr. White rarely sneaks up on me anymore. I'm feeling good. I've got you to thank for that."

"You did the heavy lifting. I just provided the pattern."

They stepped out of the shower. Nicole handed Bryan a towel

before she started drying herself. "I don't want to be gone too long. James will think he's lost me. You going to be okay?" she asked.

"I'll be fine."

"I need to know that you're going to be a good boy."

"I've got plenty of money."

"What are you going to do when you get bored?"

"Is it okay if I seduce a married woman?"

"As long as she's not part of a job."

Bryan hung up his towel. "If it's your last day, you get to choose the restaurant."

Nicole studied his face. "Are you really going to be okay?"

"I've got to say, baby, I was really worried about you after what Mr. White did to you."

"I could tell."

"Doesn't matter how tough you are, you only bounce back from so many of those."

"I know."

"I couldn't be prouder of the way you handled yourself."

She put her hands on his hips and looked up into his face. "So you want me to be safe. That's why you're going to be okay."

He kissed her. "There's no air between us. We're always skin on skin. It doesn't matter who you're with or where you're at—you're always mine. That's why I'm going to be okay. Let's get dressed and go to dinner."

DENISON STOOD on the right of way near the San Francisco Bay Trail leading up to the Golden Gate Bridge. Even though it was still early, in the midst of morning rush hour, tourists on rented bicycles, runners, and skaters all zoomed past behind him. The fog on the bay was slowly thinning, the sun cutting through it and promising a sunny afternoon. Denison sipped his coffee. This was his morning spot. He sat on a boulder and watched the seagulls ride the breeze and swoop down for edible bits. A freighter appeared out of the fog, easing along, headed for the docks. A man carrying a tripod camera walked along the edge of the water, found his spot, set up the tripod, and started taking pictures of the bridge. Denison wondered if he was any good. So many pictures of the bridge seemed pretty much the same.

"James."

He looked back up toward the street. Nicole was walking toward him, making her way through the rocks. She looked like a mirage: slave sandals, skinny jeans, a bright red, scooped-neck top, her hair loose around her shoulders. For a moment he wasn't quite sure it was really her. But it was. Not the woman who left with Bryan, but the woman he'd known at the beginning.

She walked straight into his arms and gave him the hard kiss that always says "I missed you." He breathed in her scent, then stepped back and held her by the arms as if he was afraid she would vanish into thin air. "When did you get here?"

"Just now. I let myself into your apartment. I hope you don't mind."

"I don't mind." He laughed. "That's great, in fact. How did you find me?"

She punched him playfully on the shoulder. "I have my devious ways."

"I'm so surprised. I can't stop looking at you."

"You thought I wasn't coming back."

"It had crossed my mind."

"You should have called."

"I didn't want to crowd you."

"Jimmy, really? We're closer than that."

"What do I call you now?"

"Call me? Nicole. With you I'm always Nicole."

"Have you eaten? You want to get some breakfast? There's a place near my apartment."

They walked hand-in-hand out of the park, across the street and past the nearby businesses, and into a neighborhood of narrow two- and three-story houses with privacy fences. The on-street parking was crowded with cars. Up ahead on the corner on the left was a mom-and-pop restaurant called Morning Flower Cafe. Denison held the door for her. The restaurant was mostly empty. Contemporary folk music played from speakers high up on the walls. A sign at the hostess stand said *Seat Yourself.* They sat at a table in the window.

"How's Bryan?"

"He's keeping busy. You might remember that he ran into some trouble just before he came to help us."

"Yeah."

"That was because I wasn't there to help him and his new associate wasn't up to the job. But we got that sorted out."

Their server, a thin young man wearing black pants and a white shirt with a turquoise and gold bolo tie, set menus down in front of them. They ordered coffee. Nicole looked out the window and twirled a strand of hair before she spoke again. "I was going to wait until later to talk about this, you know, after a few days of bliss, but since we're on the subject, in the interest of transparency, I guess we'll have the tough talk now." Her smile faded.

"The tough talk?"

She nodded. "I really like being with you, James."

"I really like being with you."

"And I think we're good together."

"Ditto." His heart began to pound.

"And after that crazy trouble, your kids will get behind us now."

"But?"

"But Bryan needs me. He thought he'd train somebody new, but that didn't work out."

Denison sighed. "So you're not going to stay?"

"No, silly." She swiped at the air. "I want to stay. But if we're going to be together, I need to be able to help Bryan when he needs me."

Their server brought their coffee. They ordered omelets with toast. After he left, Denison said, "Will you sleep with other guys?"

"For work?"

He nodded.

"If I have to."

"Even after what happened?"

"Rape isn't about sex."

"I know that."

"But you don't *know* it. How can you, when it's never happened to you?"

"But sleeping with guys, in your work—that can be dangerous."

"Yeah, what I do can be dangerous."

"And you still want to do it?"

"It's my choice."

"But you don't have to do it anymore. I want you to stay with me."

"That's sweet, Jimmy, and I really appreciate it, but I just can't leave Bryan in the lurch. If you want me, that's the way it's got to be."

"So I'd have to share you with him."

"If you put it that way."

"And you'd still be sleeping with him?"

She shrugged. "I won't lie to you. Not about anything important."

They were quiet while their server set their breakfast dishes down before them. "What's important?" he asked.

"Anything that's about us."

"It's crazy. I don't know how I'll feel about it in the future, but right now I want to be with you so much that I'll share you with him if that's what I have to do."

"When I'm with you, I'm only with you."

"I know."

"But when I disappear for weeks at a time, come back with a new scar and can't tell you what I've done—well, you're just going to have to trust me."

"So that's the talk?" Denison asked.

"Yes, that's the talk."

"And what about what happened to you? You seem completely like your old self. Before, you cringed when I touched you."

"Some days are worse than others, but I am doing better. It's hard to explain, but me and Bryan together, doing our thing, it heals me. Little by little I feel my confidence return, and the crazy despair goes away. It must sound weird."

"So this has happened before?"

"Do you really want to know?"

"I love you. I want to know everything about you."

They sat quietly for a while, eating their breakfasts and looking out the window onto the street. Their server cleared the dishes and brought their check.

"What do you want to do next?" he asked.

"Don't you have work?"

"It's been a month since I've seen you. I'm going to take the day."

She smiled mischievously. "Then I think we should spend the day like newlyweds, lying naked in bed and ordering delivery food. What do you think about that?"

"Maybe we should go out for a late supper. I know a little Italian place where we can get a reservation."

"That sounds great."

He reached across the table and took her hand. "I'm so glad you're here."

"Me too," she said. "Me too."

LATER THAT DAY Bryan received a text from Nicole. Everything was as it should be. He slipped his phone back into his pocket. He was watching a middle-aged woman sitting with two girlfriends at a table across the restaurant. She was wearing a bright red, short-sleeved dress and a strand of pearls. She seemed a likely prospect: outgoing, sure of herself, working on her second glass of wine. She looked amazingly like Nicole, though her gestures were different. She finally noticed he was watching her. He smiled. She smiled back. He went back to his newspaper and his Rueben sandwich, but he surreptitiously kept an eye on her. When she and her girlfriends got up to leave, he followed them. Out in front of the restaurant, he caught up to her.

"I'm sorry," he said, putting his hands into the pockets of his sports coat, "I know this sounds like the worst sort of cliché, but you look familiar to me. Have we met before?"

She shook her head. "No, I don't think so."

He put on a puzzled expression. "Really?"

"Now you're just flirting."

"Guilty as charged. I'm Doug. Doug Johnson." He stuck out his hand.

"What makes you think I'm going to tell you my name?"

"Ouch."

She smiled.

"You busy this afternoon?"

"You bored?"

"Yes. Yes, I am bored. Do you like the aquarium? I'd like to go, but I don't want to go alone."

"You're very persistent, Doug."

"Thank you."

"What do you think my husband would think of me spending the afternoon with a strange man?"

"We keep talking, and I won't be a stranger."

"And why did you choose me?"

"You really do look like an old friend of mine. She's the kind of woman who knows her own mind, likes a little adventure. I thought you might be that sort of woman too."

She folded her arms. "You are a bad boy."

"Hey, if you don't like the aquarium, we could go to the art museum, or just take a walk in the park. All nice, safe public places. Just looking for some stimulating conversation. I find that most experiences are improved by the company of an interesting woman."

"You're quite the flatterer."

"Is it flattery if it's true?"

"There's a photography museum around the corner from here on Eleventh Street. There's a new exhibit of landscapes I haven't seen, if you care for that sort of thing."

"Fantastic. Lead the way."

They started down the sidewalk, Bryan making light conversation, thinking about how much he was going to enjoy the challenge of getting her into bed. He was glad it wasn't an obvious sure thing. Hit or miss, it was going to make a great story to share with Nicole.

A NOTE FROM THE AUTHOR

Thanks for reading *The Kidnap Victim*. If you enjoyed it, please post a short review on your favorite book review site. A few words will do. Honest reviews are the number one way I attract new readers.

Thanks so much.

I'd love to hear from you. You can reach me at my website:
http://michaelpking.org

The Travelers
The Double Cross: A Travelers Prequel
The Traveling Man: Book One
The Computer Heist: Book Two
The Blackmail Photos: Book Three
The Freeport Robbery: Book Four
The Kidnap Victim: Book Five

Made in the USA
Middletown, DE
04 September 2019